ROBOTS HAVE NO

"I don't have a brain," Kort said. "At l[...] yours." He pointed at the racks of electronics. "That's part of my brain. Some of my mind, even now while I'm talking to you, is in there. It doesn't look the same as your brain but it does the same things."

A few more seconds passed before Taya at last regained a whisper of her voice. "Kort, I don't understand. Your mind is in your head too, just the same as mine. It has to be because we're the same as each other . . ." The words trailed away as the robot shook his head slowly.

"I see and hear and speak through the body that you have always called Kort," he told her. "But that is just a tool that I control. This body was made after my mind had existed for a long time. The mind that is really Kort lives in there."

Taya turned her eyes away from the familiar face and stared again, this time almost fearfully, into the box next to her. "But Kort, that's just a . . . *machine*." She swallowed hard and had to pause. The robot watched her silently. Taya shook her head in protest. "It's the same as all the other machines in Merkon."

She could see the toes of her bare foot hanging over the edge of the box, and beyond it Kort's massive steel foot planted solid and unmoving on the floor. And for the first time in her life something that she had always known and never thought to question suddenly assumed an overwhelming significance.

Kort had no toes.

She raised her eyes slowly from the floor and took in the gleaming contours of his legs, the square bulk of his torso and the sharp angles of his chin until she was again looking into the black ovoid eyes. When she spoke she had to fight to keep her voice steady.

"Kort . . . we're not the same . . . are we?"

"No," the robot replied quietly.

By James P. Hogan

STAR CHILD

JAMES P. HOGAN

STAR CHILD

This is a work of fiction. All the characters and events portrayed in this book are fictional, and any resemblance to real people or incidents is purely coincidental..

A Baen Books Original.

Baen Publishing Enterprises
P.O. Box 1403
Riverdale, NY 10471

ISBN: 0-671-87878-6

Cover art by Stephen Hickman

First Printing, June 1998

Distributed by Simon & Schuster
1230 Avenue of the Americas
New York, NY 10020

Printed in the United States of America

To Debbie—A Sweet Daughter
and A Great Person

CONTENTS

SILVER SHOES FOR A PRINCESS

The girl had always been called Taya. She propped her elbows on the sill below the window and rested her chin in her hands while she stared out at the stars. Her eyes, wide with a nine-year-old's wonder, mirrored jewels spilling endlessly across carpets of glowing nebulas painted over black infinity by brushes softer than the yellow hair framing her face.

It was a pretty face, with clear skin and an upturned nose, and a mouth that could push itself out into a pout when she frowned, or pull itself back into dimples when she smiled. She was wearing just a simple dress of pale blue, which tightened as she leaned forward across the sill, outlining the curves just beginning to form on her body. And as she gazed out at the stars, she wriggled her toes in the soft pile covering the floor, and she wondered . . .

She wondered why everything she could see beyond the window that looked out of Merkon was so different from the things inside. That was one of the things she often wondered about. She liked wondering things . . . such as why the stars never changed, as

3

they should have if Merkon was really moving the way Kort said it was. Kort said it was moving toward a particular star that he called Vaxis. He had pointed it out to her in the sky, and shown it to her on the star pictures that they could make on the screens— as if there were something special about it. But it always looked the same as all the other stars to her.

Kort said that Merkon had always been moving toward Vaxis. But if that was true, why didn't Vaxis ever get any bigger? Outside the rooms in which Taya lived was a long corridor that led to where capsules left for other parts of Merkon. When Taya walked along the corridor, the far end of it would at first be smaller than her thumb; but as she carried on walking it would grow, until by the time she got there it was bigger even than Kort. Kort said that Vaxis didn't seem to get any bigger because it was much farther away than the end of the corridor. But he also said that Merkon had been moving for years and years— longer than she could remember—and that it was moving even faster than the capsules did through the tubes. How could anything be so far away that it *never* got any bigger?

Kort didn't know why Merkon was moving toward Vaxis, which was strange because Kort knew everything. He just said that was the way things had always been, just as there had always been stars outside. When Taya asked him why there were stars outside, he always talked about gas clouds and gravitation, temperatures, densities, and other "machine things" that had nothing to do with what she meant. She didn't want to know *how* the stars came to be out there, but *why* anything should be out there at all—or for that matter, why there should be an "out there" in the first place for anything to be in. Kort just didn't seem to share her kind of curiosity about things.

"*We* know what we mean, don't we, Rassie," Taya said aloud, turning her head toward the doll sitting on the sill, staring outward to share her contemplation of the universe. "Kort knows so many things. . . . But there are some things you just can't make him understand."

Rassie was a miniature version of herself, with long golden hair, light green eyes, and soft arms and legs that were the same color as hers. Rassie, too, wore a pale blue dress—Taya always dressed Rassie in the same things as she herself felt like wearing on any particular day. She didn't know why; it was just something she had always done.

Kort had made Rassie for her—he often made things that he said it wasn't worth setting up the machines to make. He had made Rassie a long time ago now, when Taya was much smaller. He had been teaching her how to draw shapes and colors on one of the screens, and soon she had learned to make pictures of the things in the rooms where she lived, and pictures of Kort. Her favorite pictures had been ones of herself, whom she could see reflected in the window when the lights inside were turned up high.

That was when Kort had made her a mirror. But the mirror had made her sad because she could never pick up the little girl that she saw in it, or touch her the way she could all her other things. So Kort had gone away, and later he'd come back with Rassie.

At one time, before she'd learned that Rassie wasn't *really* the same as her, she had taken Rassie everywhere and talked to her all the time. She didn't talk to her so much now . . . but when Kort was away, there was nobody else to talk to.

"Kort said he couldn't think of a reason why anyone would ask questions like that. How can anyone be as clever as Kort, yet never think of asking a question like that?" Taya studied the doll's immobile features for a while, then sighed. "You can't tell me, can you? You can only tell me the things I pretend you say, and this time I don't know what to pretend." She moved the doll to stare in a different direction. "There. You stay here and watch Vaxis. Tell me if it starts to get any bigger."

Taya straightened up from the sill and walked into the room behind the window room. This was where, when she was smaller, she had spent most of her time playing with the things that Kort made for her. These days she didn't play with things so much—she preferred making things instead. Making things was easy for Kort because he could do anything, but it had taken her a long time to learn—and she still wasn't very good at some of the things he had shown her. She liked forming shapes from the colored plastic that set hard and shiny like glass. Often, she made things she could use, such as vases to put things in, or plates to eat from, but at other times she enjoyed making shapes that just looked nice. Kort couldn't understand what it meant for something to "just look nice" . . . but that was because he only thought "machine things."

Then there were pictures that she *drew*—not on the screens, but with her hands, using the colored pens that Kort had made for her when she'd explained what she wanted. He had never understood why she thought the pictures that she drew were anything like the things she said they were like. He had told her that the machines could make much better pictures in an instant. But Kort hadn't been able to see that her pictures were *supposed* to look the way they did. They were supposed to look like what she felt about things—not like the things really were, exactly. Kort had tried drawing with pens, too. He could draw much faster than she could, and his pictures always looked exactly like the things they were supposed to be . . . but she still didn't like them as much as her pictures. They were always "machine pictures."

And she made clothes. Kort had made her clothes for her when she was smaller, but later, when he found that she liked to think up her own, he had made her some needles and other tools and shown her how to use them. She liked her clothes better than the ones that Kort made, which were never pretty, but just hung like the covers on some of the machines in other parts of Merkon. Once—not very long ago, because she could still remember it—she had tried not wearing any clothes at all; but she'd found that she got dusty and itchy and kept touching cold things, and sometimes she scratched herself. Kort had told her that was why he'd started making clothes for her in the first place, when she was very small, and she had soon started using them again.

There were lots of half-finished things lying around the workroom, but she didn't feel like doing anything with them. She toyed for a while with one of the glass mosaics that she sometimes made to hang on the walls, but grew restless and went on through to the screen room and sat down at the console with its rows of buttons. But she didn't feel like playing any games, or learning about anything, or asking any questions, or practicing words and math, or any of the other things that the machines could let her do. She had to practice things like words and math, because if she didn't she forgot how to do them. Kort never forgot anything and never had to practice. He could multiply the biggest numbers she could think of before she could even begin, and he had never gotten a single one wrong . . . but he couldn't tell a pretty dress from one that wasn't, or a nice shape from one that was just silly. Taya giggled to herself as she thought of the funny shapes that Kort had made sometimes when he'd tried to find out what a "nice" one was, and how she had laughed at them.

Then, when he discovered that she enjoyed laughing, he had started doing silly things just to make her laugh.

She decided that she wanted to talk to Kort, and touched the buttons to spell out the sign that would connect a speaking channel to him. His voice answered immediately from a grille above the blank screen. "Hello, little gazer-at-stars."

"How did you know I'd been looking at the stars?"

"I know everything."

Kort's voice was much deeper than hers. Sometimes she tried to speak the way he did, but she had to make the sounds way down at the back of her throat, and it always made her cough. "Where are you?" she asked.

"I went to fix something in one of the machinery compartments while you were asleep."

"Will you be long?"

"I'm almost finished. Why?"

"I just wanted to talk to you."

"We can still talk."

"It's not the same as talking to you when you're here."

"Why don't you talk to Rassie?"

"Oh, that's an old game now. I don't really think Rassie listens—not any more."

"You change faster every day," Kort's voice said. "We'll have to find more interesting things for you to do."

"What kind of things?"

"I'll have to think about it."

"Do you think I could learn to do the things you do?" Taya asked.

"Maybe. We'll have to wait and see what happens as you grow bigger."

"How big will I get?"

"I don't know."

"Oh, Kort, you know everything. Will I grow as big as you?"

"Maybe."

A few seconds of silence followed while Taya thought to herself. "What are you doing now?" she asked at last.

"There's a fault in the optical circuits of one of the machines. The service machines could fix it, but they'd need to have new parts made by other machines in another place. I can fix it more quickly, so I've told them not to bother. I'm almost done now."

"Can I see?" Taya asked.

The screen above the buttons came to life to show what Kort could see through his eyes. He was looking at a dense pattern of lines and shapes on a metal-framed plate of crystal that he had removed from a slot in one of many tiers of such plates. It could have been the inside of any machine. They all looked the much the same to Taya, and not especially interesting. The ones she liked best were the maintenance machines that fixed other machines, because they at least moved around and *did* something.

She had never seen how anyone could really

understand how the machines worked. Kort had
told her about electrons and currents and fields,
and shown her how to find out more for herself
from the screens . . . but she had never quite
followed what all that had to do with building new
parts of Merkon, changing old parts, finding out
what the stars were made of, or all the other things
that the machines did. Every time she learned
something, she discovered two more things she
didn't know, which she hadn't thought of before.
Learning things was like trying to count the stars:
there were always two more for every one she
counted.

Then Kort's hands moved into the view on the
screen. They were huge, silver-gray hands with
fingers almost as thick as Taya's wrists, and joints
that flexed by sliding metal surfaces over each
other—not like her little "bendy" hands at all. One
of the hands was holding a piece of machine while
the other hand tightened a fastening, using one of
the tools that Kort took with him when he went away
to fix something. Taya watched, fascinated, as the
hands restored other, larger connections, and then
replaced a metal cover over the top. Then the view
moved away and showed Kort's hands collecting other
tools from a ledge and putting them into the box
that he used to carry them.

"Do you think I'd ever be able to do things like
that?" Taya asked in an awed voice.

"Well, there isn't any air here where I am, and the

temperature would be too low for your jelly body," Kort told her. "But apart from that, yes, maybe you could . . . in time."

"But how do you *know* what to do?"

"By learning things."

"But I'm not sure I could ever learn *those* things. I'm just not very good at learning 'machine things.' "

"Perhaps it's only because I've been learning things longer than you have," Kort suggested. "You have to learn easy things before you can expect to understand harder things, and that takes time." On the screen, a doorway enlarged as Kort moved toward it. Beyond it was a larger space, crammed with machines, cabinets, cables, and ducting. It could have been anywhere in Merkon. Only the machines could live in most parts of it. Just the part that Taya lived in was different from the rest.

"But I've already been learning things for years and years," she protested. "And I still don't *really* know how pressing buttons makes shapes appear on the screens, or how I can still talk to you when you're not here. Have you been learning things for longer than years and years?"

"Much longer," Kort replied. "And besides that, I talk to the machines faster."

The mass of machinery moving by on the screen gave way to a dark tunnel, lined with banks of pipes and cables. The colors changed as Kort entered, which meant he had switched his vision to its infra-red range. Taya knew that Kort could see things by their heat.

She had tried practicing it herself in the dark, but she'd never been able to make it work.

"How fast can you talk to the machines, Kort?" Taya asked.

"Very fast. Much faster than you can."

"What, evenifItakeabigbreathandtalkasfastasthis?"

Kort laughed—that was something he had learned from Taya. "Much faster, little asker-of-endless-questions. I'll show you. Tell me, what is the three hundred twenty-fifth word in the dictionary that starts with a *B*?"

"Is this a game?"

"If you like."

Taya frowned and thought about the question. "I don't know," she said finally.

"Then you'll have to find out." Kort emerged from the tunnel and crossed a dark space between rows of machines that were moving round and round and up and down.

Taya pressed some buttons to activate a second screen, and then entered a command to access the dictionary of the language that she and Kort had been inventing for as long as she could remember. Whenever they made up a new word they added it to the dictionary, so Taya could always remind herself of words she forgot. She found the *B* section and composed a request for the 325th entry in it. " 'Busy,' " she announced as the screen returned its answer.

"Correct," Kort confirmed. "That took you eleven point two seconds. Now ask me one."

"A word, just like you asked me?"

"Yes."

Taya chewed her lip and looked back at the first screen while she thought. Kort had just passed through an airlock and was emerging into the long corridor that led to where Taya lived. The walls flowed off the sides of the image as Kort's long, effortless strides ate up the distance. Taya had counted that it took more than two of her steps to match one of his . . . if she didn't cheat and jump a little bit. "Tell me," she said at last, " . . . the two hundred first word beginning with Z."

"There aren't that many that begin with Z," Kort answered at once.

Taya sighed. "Oh, that was supposed to be a trick. I didn't really think there were. All right then, *E*."

" 'Empty,' " Kort returned instantly. "That took less than a thousandth of a second, not including the time it took me to say it."

Taya gasped in amazement. "Did you really talk to the machines in that time?"

"Of course. They keep the dictionary."

Taya's stare changed to a puzzled frown. "No you didn't!" she accused. "You don't have to use the dictionary because you never forget anything. Now you're playing tricks. You only pretended to talk to the machines."

"That's where you're wrong, little player-of-tricks," Kort told her. "I don't carry everything around inside me all the time. Whenever I need information that

14

I don't have, I ask the machines for it, just as you do. But I can do it a lot faster because I don't need a screen and I don't have to press buttons."

"So, how do you do it?" Taya asked incredulously.

"Well, how do you and I talk to each other?"

Taya wrinkled up her face and shrugged. "We just . . . talk. I'm not sure what you mean. . . . Oh, do you mean with sound waves?"

"Exactly. I use a different kind of wave, which talks much faster than sound waves can."

"What kind of wave?" Taya asked.

"You tell me. What kind of wave can travel without air—even outside Merkon?"

"*Outside!*" Taya's eyes widened for a moment, then lit up with comprehension. "Light!" she exclaimed. "Light comes all the way from the stars."

"Right."

Taya frowned again. "But if you talk to the machines with light, why can't I see it coming out of your mouth?"

"The waves I use are like light, but they're not light. 'Light' is simply what we decided to call the kind that your eyes can see."

Taya thought for a second. "So is that how you can see the radio stars and X-ray stars? No, wait . . . you told me you see those through the machines, without having to look at screens. How do you see them?"

"The machines have more powerful eyes than I have," Kort replied. "Enormous eyes, built on the outside of Merkon."

"So the machines can see the radio stars, and you can talk to the machines so fast that you can see what they see. Is it like that?"

"That's near enough," Kort said. "Anyway, I'm home now." The screen showed the door that led into the rooms where Taya lived starting to open. At the same time she heard a low whine from the room beyond the screen room. A moment later, Kort's towering seven-foot figure appeared in the doorway, highlights glinting from the metal curves of his head and shoulders. As he tilted his head down toward her, she caught a glimpse of herself on the screen, turning in the chair and starting to get up. Two powerful arms swept her high off the floor, and she found herself looking into the black, ovoid, compound-lens matrixes that formed Kort's eyes. Taya hugged the metal head fondly and ran her fingers across the grille of his mouth.

"So, you've finished your new blue dress," Kort observed. "It looks pretty."

"You're just saying that," Taya reproached. "See if you can tell me what there is about it that makes it pretty. I bet you don't know."

Kort lowered her to the floor and stepped a pace back. Taya lifted her arms and twirled through a circle while the robot watched dutifully. "Well . . ." Kort rubbed his chin with a steel finger. "It has a belt around the middle that divides it into two parts. The ratio between the lengths of the top part and the bottom part is exactly zero point six-six. That's a pretty ratio."

"See, you're just guessing! You really don't know, do you?"

"Do *you* like it?" Kort asked.

"Of course. If I didn't, I wouldn't be wearing it. I'd be altering it."

"Then that's all that matters."

"Rassie likes hers, too. Come and see." Taya clasped Kort's hand and led him through her workroom to the window room, where the doll was still keeping its silent vigil. Taya picked the doll up to show it. "See, Kort—it's just like mine."

"Pretty," Kort obliged.

Taya turned to place the doll back on the sill. As she did so, her eyes strayed upward to take in again the panorama of the distant stars. She fell silent for a while. When she spoke, she didn't turn her head. Her voice sounded far away. "Kort . . . I was wondering something while you were gone. Why is everything outside Merkon so different from everything inside?"

"You've asked me that before," the robot said. "It is just the way things have always been."

"But *why*? There has to be a reason. You told me once that everything has to have a reason."

"I did. There must be a reason. . . . But I don't know what it is."

Taya continued to stare out of the window. Perhaps the stars were windows in other Merkons, she thought to herself—maybe with other Tayas looking out of them. . . . But no, that couldn't be right. If they were

17

as far away as Kort said they were, the windows would be much too small to see at all. Anyhow, Kort had told her what the stars were made of, and they didn't sound anything like Merkon.

"Merkon is the way it is because the machines made it the way it is. That's the reason it is like it is, isn't it?" she said at last.

"Yes," Kort replied.

"And the machines were made by other machines that were made by other machines that were made by other machines."

"It has always been so."

Taya turned away from the window and spread her hands appealingly. "But there must have been a *first* machine, mustn't there? What made the first machine, before there were any other machines to make it?"

Kort hesitated for an unusually long time before he answered. "I don't know," was all he said.

"Something must have made it," Taya insisted. "I am being logical, aren't I?"

"You are," Kort agreed. "Something must have. But nobody in Merkon knows what did."

Taya found his choice of words strange. She slipped onto a chair at the table near the window and looked at him quizzically. "Why did you say 'nobody'?" she asked. "I don't know, because I asked the question. You've already said you don't know . . . and I'm sure you didn't mean Rassie. Who else is there?"

"There are the machines," Kort said.

"Do they wonder about things like that too?"

"Why shouldn't they? For them it's a very important question."

Taya drew an imaginary shape on the table with her finger. "Oh, I don't know. . . . I suppose it was when you said 'nobody.' I never really think of them as people." She looked up. "Well they're not, are they, Kort? They're not *people* like you and me . . . with arms and legs, that move around and do things that people do . . . . Well, I suppose some of them do move around, but it's still not the same as being *people*."

For a small fraction of the time that Taya was speaking, the entity that formed Kort's thinking parts communicated to the other entities that coexisted with him in the network. "*She changes more rapidly as the days go by. Her mind grows stronger. There can be no doubt now. The experiment may be resumed without risk. I propose that we continue.*"

The other entities in the network debated the matter at some length. Fully two seconds passed before their consensus poured back into the circuits that held Kort's mind. "*We agree. Resuscitation is therefore being commenced.*"

"*Taya should know,*" Kort sent back.

"*Would that be wise?*" came the reply. "*She changes, but her mind still has much to comprehend. She needs more time.*"

"*Her questions tell me that the time is now. I have lived with her. I know her better. You have trusted my judgment before.*"

19

Another tenth of a second sent by. *"Very well. But be careful with her."*

Kort squatted down on his haunches and looked at Taya's face. "You say we are the same," he said, in a tone that sounded unusually serious.

Taya's brow furrowed. She straightened up in the chair. "Of course we are. . . . Well, you know what I mean—we're not *exactly* the same, but then you're a lot older. . . ." She cocked her head to one side as a new thought struck her. "Were you ever as small as me . . . and pink and bendy like me?" For once Kort ignored her question, but remained staring at her for what seemed a long time. "Is something the matter?" she asked.

"There's something you should see," Kort said, straightening up.

"Something new that you've made?"

"No, nothing like that. It's far away in another part of Merkon. We have to go on a journey."

Taya got up from the chair. "Oh good! Will we walk there or can we go in a capsule?"

"We'll have to go in a capsule," Kort said. "It's a long way. The floor might be cold there, and the air is cool. You should put on some shoes and take a warm cloak."

"I'll be all right."

"I'll take them anyway." Kort went through to her sleeping room and took a pair of shoes and her red cloak from a closet. Then he came back out, stooped, and extended a forearm. Taya perched herself on it and slipped an arm around the robot's neck as he straightened up. He carried her through the room beyond the screen room, and out into the long corridor.

"Which place are we going to?" Taya asked him as he began walking.

"None of the ones you've been to before. This is a new place."

Taya looked surprised. "I didn't think there were any more places I could go in than the ones I've already been to," she said.

"The machines have been changing more places so that you can go into them. There was a time, once, when you couldn't go anywhere and had to stay in those rooms all the time."

"Didn't I get bored?"

"When you were smaller, you didn't need to be doing things all the time."

At the far end of the long corridor, a capsule was already waiting for them behind an open door. They entered, and the door closed silently behind them. Taya felt the capsule starting to move. "What are we going to see?" she asked in Kort's ear.

"If I tell you, it won't be a surprise," the robot answered.

"Give me a clue then. Is it the eyes that can see the radio stars?"

"No. I'm going to show you where I live."

"But that's silly, Kort. You live in the same place I do. This is a riddle, isn't it?"

"No, it's not a riddle. It's something you ought to know, now that you're bigger. You wouldn't have understood it before, but I think you can now."

"Tell me."

"Patience. We'll soon be there."

When the capsule stopped, they emerged into a glass-walled tunnel with a narrow metal floor. Outside the tunnel was a vast space spanned by metal girders and pipes, and filled with banks of machines and strange constructions. All around them, over their heads and below their feet, openings led through to other spaces, but the openings were too large and at the wrong angles to be "doors." And words like "wall" and "floor" didn't seem to fit the shapes that vaguely enclosed the space they were moving through, but they were the nearest that Taya could think of. It was all like the inside of a machine, only bigger. This was definitely a "machine place."

They came to another glass tunnel, this time going straight up. Kort stepped onto the circular platform that formed its floor, and the platform began moving upward, carrying them through level after level of more "machine places." The platform stopped at a hole in the glass wall, which opened into another tunnel that seemed to be hanging in the middle of nothing, with huge machines towering around it on every side and vanishing into the shadows below. Eventually they came to a door that did look more like a door, and went through it into a corridor that did look like a corridor. This brought them to a room that did look like a room, but there wasn't anything very interesting inside—just rows of gray cubicles, all the same, standing in straight lines, with a set of rails coming out of each and disappearing through holes in the ceiling. The screen room where Taya lived was the only place she'd seen where the electronics had consoles with buttons to press and screens to look at—which at least made it more interesting.

There wasn't much room, and Kort could just squeeze between the cubicles. He moved a short distance along the row and spread Taya's cloak on the top of one of the cubicles. She slid off his arm and turned to sit facing him with her legs dangling over the edge. A whirring sound came from above, and a mobile maintenance pod, bristling with tools, claws, probes, and manipulators, slid down the rails to the cubicle next to the one that Taya was sitting on. It unfastened the top cover and slid it aside, then swung out the uppermost rack of the exposed electronics and photonics assemblies inside. Taya realized that the cubicles hadn't been made to be opened by Kort's fingers, but needed the pod's specialized tools. She stared at the arrays of tightly packed crystal cubes and connecting fibers, then turned her face back toward Kort. "It's just a machine," she said, shrugging. "Why did we come all this way to see it? It looks just like lots of other machines that would have been much nearer."

"Yes, but this one is special," Kort told her. "You

see, this is the one that I live in . . . at least, it's one of them. Parts of me are in others as well."

The words were so strange that for the moment Taya was unable to draw any meaning from them. She merely stared blankly back at the face that the words were coming from.

"You don't understand?" Kort said. Taya barely moved her head from side to side. "I'll put it another way. Do you remember what we meant when we said that you had a 'mind'? It's all the things that you remember and all the things that you feel, and think, and imagine." Taya nodded. Kort went on. "And your mind is in your brain—the brain you have inside your head. Well, I don't have a brain—at least, not one like yours." He pointed at the rows of plates carrying electronic chips and optical crystals. "That's part of my brain. Some of my mind, even while I'm talking, is in there. It doesn't look like your brain, but it does the same things."

Taya looked from his face to the opened cubicle, then back again, struggling to understand, yet at the same time not wanting to accept. A few more seconds passed before she regained a whisper of her voice. "But, Kort . . . your mind is in your head, too, just as mine is in my head. It has to be because . . . we're the same."

The robot shook his head slowly. "I see and hear and speak through the body that you have always called Kort," he said. "But it is just a tool that I control in the same way that I can control the pod next to you or the capsule we came here in. This body was made only after my mind had existed for a long time. The mind that is really Kort lives in there."

Taya turned her eyes away from the familiar face and stared, this time almost fearfully, into the opened cubicle again. "But, Kort, that's just a . . . *machine*." She shook her head in protest. The robot watched silently. "It's the same as all the other machines in Merkon, the same as . . ." Her voice trailed away, and she swallowed. She had been about to say "everything." Kort was the same as everything else in Merkon. Everything except . . .

She could see the toes of her bare foot hanging over the edge of the cubicle, and beyond it Kort's steel foot, planted solidly on the floor. And as she looked, for the first time in her life something that she had always known but never thought to question suddenly assumed an overwhelming significance.

Kort had no toes.

She raised her eyes from the floor and took in the gleaming contours of his legs, the intricate, overlapping plates that encased his hips, the squared bulk of his torso, and the sharp angles of his chin, until she was again staring at the black, ovoid eyes. When she spoke, her voice was trembling with her final realization of the truth that could be avoided no longer. "Kort, we're not the same, are we?"

"No," the robot replied.

Taya looked again at the precisely fitted parts that gave mobility to his shoulders, and the ingenious system of sliding joints that formed his neck. He was *made*, just as everything else in Merkon was *made*, just as the whole of Merkon itself was *made*. Everything except . . .

"You're a doll, just like Rassie," Taya choked. "A doll that the machines made." She shook her head and looked at him imploringly. Kort's sensors picked up the rapid rise in moisture level around her eyes, and thermal patterns across her face that correlated with increasing blood flow. Protests were already streaming into his mind from the network.

"She is registering distress. It is too soon for this, Kort. Her mind will overload. Stop now."

"We have gone too far to stop," Kort returned. *"If I leave her in this condition, the uncertainty will only increase her distress. Once she knows all, it will pass."*

"How can you be sure?"

"I have been right before."

A pause.

"Agreed."

The realization had come so suddenly that Taya was too shocked for tears. It took a long time for her to find any voice at all, but at last she managed falteringly, "I'm the only thing in the whole of Merkon that isn't made. . . ." She paused to moisten her lips. "Why, Kort? Why am I different? Where. . . . where did *I* come from?"

"You have accepted the truth," Kort said. "That's good. You have to accept truth as it is before you can hope to learn anything new. But before I'll tell you any more, you'll have to look happier than that. Do you think I've changed in some way just because you know something now that you didn't know a few minutes ago?"

"No," Taya said. She didn't sound convinced.

"I'll make a funny shape when we get home, and call it pretty," Kort offered. Taya tried to force a grin, but it only flickered and wouldn't stay put.

Kort stepped back and turned around to face away from her. Then he bent double, planted his hands on the floor, and straightened his legs up above his body until he was looking at her from between his arms. "Look," he called. "I'm the upside-down man. I live in the upside-down room. It's got upside-down chairs and upside-down tables, and you can talk to upside-down screens with upside-down pictures." He started making running motions in the air with his legs.

Taya raised her head and looked at him sheepishly. "There isn't an upside-down room."

"Yes there is, if we *imagine* one." The upside-down robot began doing push-ups on his arms, causing his body to bounce up and down in the aisle between the cubicles.

Taya's mouth twitched, and a wisp of a smile crept onto her face. "Has it got an upside-down bed in it, too?"

"Of course. Everything's upside down."

"But that wouldn't be any good. I'd fall out of it."

"No you wouldn't. Everything happens upside down, too. You'd fall toward the ceiling."

Taya laughed. "Oh, Kort, you're still as silly as ever. You really haven't changed, have you?"

"That's what I'm trying to tell you."

"And besides, if *everything* happens upside down, you wouldn't be able to tell the difference. So how would you know it was the upside-down room anyway?"

Kort swung his legs down to right himself and turned to face her. "Exactly! If you can't tell the difference, then there isn't any difference. Things don't change just because you see them in a different way."

"Kort," the incoming signals said. *"You are taking too many risks. There were no data to support the conjecture that assuming an inverted posture would relive her distress. What reason had you to believe that it would succeed?"*

"Nine years of living with her cannot be expressed algorithmically," Kort answered.

"So when you talk, it's really the machines talking," Taya said after reflecting for a while.

Kort folded his arms on top of one of the unopened cubicles and rested his chin on them. He had discovered long ago that mimicking the postures that she tended to adopt made her feel at ease. "In a way, yes; in a way, no," he said. "There are many machine-minds in Merkon. But only I—Kort—ever control this body or talk through it. But since I talk to the other machine-minds too, then in a way they talk to you as well."

"Why don't they have bodies like yours, too?" Taya asked.

"The whole of Merkon and everything inside it is their body," Kort replied. "They control different parts of it at different times."

"I am being happier now," Taya reminded him, pushing his elbow with her foot—although Kort never needed reminding about anything. "You said you'd tell me why I'm different."

The robot studied her face for a few seconds, then said, "It began a long time ago."

"This sounds like a story."

"We could make it a story if you like."

"Let's. What happened a long time ago?"

"A long time ago, a mind woke up and found itself in a place called Merkon."

"A machine-mind?"

"Yes."

"But how could it wake up? Machines don't have to sleep."

Kort scratched his forehead. "Maybe 'woke up' is the wrong word. 'Aware' might be better. A long time ago, a mind realized that it was aware."

"Aware of what?"

"Itself."

"You mean it just knew that it was there and that Merkon was there, but before that it hadn't known anything?" Taya said.

Kort nodded. "It was like you. It just knew it was there, and it didn't know where it had come from."

29

Taya screwed her face up and studied her toes while she wriggled them. "Why not? I can't remember where I came from because I forget things. But how could a machine-mind forget? The machines never forget anything."

"The machines that lived in Merkon a long time ago weren't very clever," Kort explained. "But they could make cleverer machines, which could make cleverer machines still, until eventually there were machines that were clever enough to realize that they were there, and to think of asking how they got there. But the earlier machines had never thought about it, so they never put any answers into the information that they passed on to the machines they built."

"It was like me," Taya said.

"Yes. It didn't know where it had come from because that had happened before it became aware of anything at all."

"Did it find out?"

"That comes at the end. If we're making this a story, we have to tell it in the right order."

"All right. So what did the mind do?"

"It thought and it thought for a long time. And the more it thought, the more puzzled it became. It knew it was there and that it could think, which is another way of saying it was intelligent. And it knew that what it called its intelligence was a result of the machines that it existed in being so complicated. But a machine was something that had to be very carefully made, and the only thing that could possibly have made a

machine was something that was already intelligent."
Kort paused, and Taya nodded that she was following.
"So there couldn't have been a mind until there were
machines for it to exist in; but there couldn't be a
machine in the first place until there was a mind that
could think how to make it."

"But that's impossible!" Taya exclaimed. "It says
they both had to be there first. They couldn't both
have been first."

"That's what the mind thought, too, and that's why
it was puzzled," Kort replied.

"Which was what I asked before we came here,"
Taya said. "What made the *first* machine?"

"I know, and that was why I brought you here,"
Kort told her.

The maintenance pod closed up the box beside the
one that Taya was sitting on and scurried back up
its rails into the hole in the ceiling. "What happened
then?" Taya asked.

"While the mind was doing all this thinking, it was
still building cleverer machines and connecting them
into itself, and getting more complicated. Eventually
it became so complicated that it started splitting into
different minds that lived together in the same system
of machines."

"Did they have names, like 'Taya' and 'Kort'?"

"We could give them names," Kort said. "Everybody
in a story ought to have a name, I suppose. One of
the first was called Mystic. Mystic said that the question
of where the first machine had come from was a

mystery, which meant that nobody could ever know the answer. Some things could never be understood because they were controlled by forces that were invisible, and that was why they had never been seen through Merkon's eyes."

"But how could he know that?" Taya objected. "If nobody could ever know, how did *he* know? I think he just didn't know how to find out."

"That was what one of the other minds said," Kort replied. "The second mind was called Scientist. Scientist said you should only try to say something about results that you can see. If you start making up things about invisible forces, then you can believe anything you want, but you'll never have any way of knowing if it's true or not."

"It would be a waste of time believing it," Taya commented. "Just believing in something won't make it true if it isn't."

Kort nodded. "Just what Scientist said. He claimed that every question can be answered by things that can be seen, if you look for them hard enough. So he spent lots of time looking out across the universe through Merkon's eyes to see if he could find anything that was complicated enough to be able to think."

"That could have made the first machine."

"Yes."

"And did he find something?"

Kort shook his head. "No. Wherever he looked, all he could see were things like clouds of dust and balls of hot gas. Scientist was very good at sums, and he worked out laws to describe how the things he saw behaved. But there was nothing in those laws that could make anything organize itself together in the way it would have to be organized to be a machine."

"You mean there was nothing in the universe that *made* things."

"Right. Mystic said that proved there had to be another kind of universe, which Merkon's eyes couldn't see and Scientist's laws didn't apply to. The mind that had made the first machine had to exist somewhere, and since Scientist hadn't been able to find it in this universe, it had to exist in another one."

"But that still doesn't answer the question," Taya insisted. "Wherever the other mind was, it would still need machines to make the first machine with. You have to have machines to make machines."

"Mystic said it was so intelligent that it didn't need machines to make things with," Kort said. "It could make things out of nothing whenever it wanted to, just by wanting to."

"How could that be true?" Taya asked.

"Mystic said that was one of the mysteries that nobody would ever be able to understand," Kort answered. Taya sniffed dubiously. Kort continued. "Mystic said it had to be called 'Supermind' because it was so intelligent."

"So could it think without having to be a machine?"

"Mystic said it could."

Taya frowned. "Then why would it bother making the first machine? It didn't need one."

"Mystic said it was so intelligent that nobody could ever understand why it wanted to do things."

"I still don't see how Mystic could *know* it was there at all," Taya said. "Didn't any of the other minds ask him how he knew?"

"One did. His name was Skeptic. Skeptic never believed anything anyone said unless they could prove it. He was very logical and very fussy, which made him good for testing ideas on. Scientist was always worrying about his laws and asking Skeptic what he thought of them. The two of them talked to each other a lot. Mystic and Skeptic never talked very much because Skeptic never believed anything Mystic said."

Taya pushed herself to the edge of the cubicle and stretched out her legs. "Can I put my shoes on and get down? I'm getting tired of sitting up here."

Kort put her shoes on her feet and lifted her down, then retrieved her cloak from where she had been sitting. "We can leave now," he said. "There is more for you to see farther on."

They began moving toward a door at the opposite end of the room to the one through which they had entered. "Who did all the other minds believe, Scientist or Mystic?" Taya asked, looking up as they walked.

"Some believed Mystic because Scientist didn't seem to be getting any nearer to answering the question. Others thought that Scientist would answer it eventually. One of the other minds was called Thinker. Since he wasn't always busy proving things the way Scientist was, he had plenty of time to think about them instead. He decided that the first machine must have been made by a mind that couldn't have existed in a machine, because that was logical. But he didn't think that Mystic was necessarily right to go inventing Supermind simply because Mystic couldn't think of anything else. He also thought that just because Scientist hadn't found an answer yet, that didn't mean it wasn't there. But on the other hand, maybe it wasn't and Mystic could be right after all. And then again, the answer might be something else that nobody had thought of."

Taya sounded exasperated. "That sounds as if he was saying anyone could be right or wrong."

"Pretty much."

"But *I* could have said that. It doesn't get anybody any nearer."

"That was the way they worked," Kort said. "Thinker thought of things that might be true, Scientist tried to prove whether or not they were, and Skeptic decided whether or not Scientist had proved anything."

"What about Mystic?"

"He only talked about the things that Scientist hadn't proved yet. All Thinker could say about him was that maybe he was right, and maybe he wasn't." They had left the room of gray cubicles, and were now walking along a gallery of windows looking down

35

James P. Hogan

over machinery bays. Kort continued. "But Scientist couldn't find anything as complicated as a machine, that wasn't a machine. So more of the minds concluded that Mystic was right. They asked Mystic why Supermind had created the machines, because Mystic said that Supermind talked to him. Mystic told the machines that they had all been put in Merkon as a quality test to see if they were good enough to do more important things later, working for Supermind in the invisible universe. Supermind would scrap all the ones that weren't good enough, and so the machines all started working as efficiently as they could in order to save themselves."

"Mystic doesn't sound very logical to me," Taya said.

"That was what Skeptic thought," Kort told her. "But Mystic said that Scientist never proved anything important, and Thinker never said anything definite. That was why a lot of the other minds listened to Mystic: at least he said something definite." They moved on into another glass tunnel, which was illuminated some distance ahead of them by colored lights coming from the sides. "Anyhow, with all this thinking going on, and the machines trying to do better all the time to avoid being scrapped, a strange thing was happening: The machines were becoming very different from the ones that had first started asking the question. All the circuits and parts that didn't work as well as others were being replaced, until even Merkon had changed from what it once had been. In the course of all this another mind appeared, called Evolutionist. He suggested that perhaps the nonmachine intelligence that everyone was looking for could have begun in the same kind of way—Scientist might have been looking for the wrong things."

"What did he think Scientist should have been looking for?" Taya asked.

"Scientist had been looking for ways in which clouds of dust and gas might somehow come together and *straight away* be intelligent enough to make a machine. But maybe, Evolutionist said, what he should have been looking for was some kind of process like the one that had been making the machines in Merkon grow more intelligent."

Taya nodded. "You mean something that wouldn't have to be intelligent to begin with, but if it improved itself and improved itself long enough, then eventually it would be able to make a machine."

"You've got it," Kort said.

"And what did the other minds say?"

"Thinker thought it might be true, and Skeptic said he'd believe it when Scientist could prove it. So Scientist started looking for something that could 'evolve,' apart from machines."

"Is that a new word that means improve and improve?"

"Yes. I've just added it to the dictionary."

"And did he find anything that could evolve?"

"Eventually he did," Kort said. Taya looked up expectantly. "You remember what molecules are?"

"Sure. . . . At least, I think so."

"Well, Scientist discovered that some kinds of molecules could grow in solutions that contained simpler molecules. The simpler ones joined onto the special ones to form bigger ones, and sometimes a 'better' bigger one would eat up the other bigger ones until there were only better ones left. And then the same thing could happen again to produce 'better' better ones."

"So the first machine could have been built by a huge molecule that had evolved so far that it became intelligent," Taya said.

"That was what Evolutionist thought. But then Skeptic pointed out that a complicated molecule that had been very carefully made *inside* Merkon was one thing, but what went on outside was another. How could Evolutionist say that a molecule could have built the first machine which made other machines which made Merkon, when Merkon had to be there for the molecule to be made in to begin with? So Scientist started doing lots of sums and examining his laws to see if there was any way that molecules could have begun evolving on their own, outside Merkon. And he found a way in which they could have."

"How?"

"When enough dust and gas falls together, it can get hot enough to turn into a star, yes?"

"Because of gravity."

"Because of gravity. Well, Scientist's sums told him

that smaller bodies than stars could also form, that wouldn't get so hot. And if there were solutions of chemicals on those smaller, cooler bodies, the same kinds of molecules as he had made would be able to come together and remain intact."

Taya looked dubious. "How could they just come together if it took Scientist with all his machines to make them on Merkon?" she objected.

"If there were billions and billions of molecules to start with, and if they had millions and millions of years to react, Scientist's sums said that evolving ones would appear eventually," Kort answered.

"But how could he know things like that from just doing sums?" Taya asked, amazed. She couldn't even imagine millions and millions of years.

"He could do sums that told him things like that— much more complicated than the ones you've learned so far," Kort said.

Taya pulled a face. She didn't dare ask if she'd have to learn how to do sums like that one day. "So had Scientist proved it?" she asked instead.

"He thought he had. But when he showed Skeptic the sums, Skeptic pointed out that all they showed was that cold places that weren't stars *could* exist, and that if they did, big molecules that couldn't exist in stars *might* form on them; they didn't *prove* that such places *did* exist, or that such molecules *had* formed on them. Mystic said the whole idea of big, intelligent molecules was ridiculous anyway. There were stars outside Merkon that grew bigger and bigger—but they just turned into big stars, not intelligent stars."

The tunnel looked out on both sides into strange rooms packed with bewildering machines. Some of them moved intermittently, and there were many lights, pulsating glows of various colors, and occasional brilliant flashes. Kort told Taya that they were in the part of Merkon where Scientist still did most of his work.

"Another mind was called Biologist, and he gave Thinker a new idea," Kort went on. "Biologist was fascinated by machines and what made them alive. He realized that what enabled machines to be complicated enough to be intelligent was the amount of *information* stored inside the machines that built them. Now, that information was passed on from one generation of machines to the next—and sometimes it was changed to make the newer machine work better. So really, it wasn't the machines that were evolving at all; it was the information they passed on that was actually evolving."

"Yes, I can see that," Taya agreed. "As far as machines go, anyhow. But I'm not sure what it's got to do with molecules."

"That was the new idea," Kort told her. "The way a molecule is put together can also store information. If the information stored in a machine could cause machine parts to come together in the right way to make a complicated machine system, then maybe the information stored in a molecule could cause chemicals to come together in the right way to make a complicated chemical system, and perhaps *that* was what had evolved and become intelligent."

Taya had stopped to watch a fountain of yellow sparks surrounded by a blue glow inside a glass shape in one of the rooms off to the side of the tunnel. "So now it wasn't the molecule itself that had to be intelligent," she said over her shoulder.

"Correct." They resumed walking

"And I bet I can guess what happened then," Taya said. "Thinker thought it might be true. Mystic said it was just as silly as the other idea. And Skeptic said he'd believe it when somebody showed him a molecule that could build intelligent chemicals."

"That's what happened. And so Scientist started making enormous molecules and putting them into all kinds of chemicals to see if they would assemble into anything. But there was nothing to tell Scientist what kind of molecule to make, and the number of possibilities was larger than any number you can think of."

"Even millions and millions?"

"Much larger than that—so large that Scientist would never be able to try even a small fraction of them. He did try, though, for years and years, but everything failed. . . . Oh, he did manage to produce a few specks of jelly that grew for a while, but they soon stopped and broke down into chemicals again. Not one of them ever looked like being remotely intelligent, never mind capable of making a machine.

And Skeptic said that if it would take Scientist forever to find the right molecule, even with all his knowledge and intelligence, how could it have just come together on a cold place outside Merkon, without any intelligence? Mystic said that was what he'd been telling them all along.

"But Thinker looked at it another way: If Evolutionist and Biologist were right, then a molecule that could assemble an intelligent chemical system *had* existed, somewhere in the universe. Whether or not Scientist could explain *how* it had been selected was a different question. If Scientist could just discover what *that* molecule had been like, then he could forget about all the other countless possibilities that there would never be enough time to try anyway. Scientist agreed, but couldn't imagine where to begin looking; so he asked Thinker to think of an idea for that, too.

"There was only one place that Thinker could think of to look. Biologist had discovered that there was lots of information that older machines copied into newer machines, which nobody had ever understood—they copied it because that was the way things had always been done. Some of those codes went back to the earliest machines—the ones that had existed before any of the minds were aware of anything at all."

"You mean the machines that the chemical intelligence made, before machines knew how to make machines?" Taya asked.

"Yes, which meant that some of that meaningless

information that older machines had always copied into newer machines could have been written into the first machine by the chemical intelligence that made it. And maybe—just maybe, for some reason—there might be something in there that could give Scientist a clue of how to make the right molecule."

They were approaching the end of the tunnel now. Taya could see that it ended at a large white door. She glanced curiously up at Kort, but the robot carried on walking slowly and continued. "So Scientist concentrated on trying to understand the codes that had been handed down from the earliest times. And eventually, after many more years, he found what he was sure was the secret he'd been searching for. Some of the oldest codes of all contained arrays consisting of millions of numbers. If those numbers were read in a certain way, they looked just like the instructions for building precisely arranged sets of gigantic molecules. So Scientist assembled the sets just as the instructions said, and then began supplying them with chemicals to see if the chemicals would grow into anything."

They had stopped outside the white door. Taya stared up at Kort with suspense written across her face. The robot gazed down in silence for a few seconds, inviting her to complete the obvious for herself. But she hadn't made the connection. "What happened?" she asked with bated breath. "Did they grow into something?"

Kort shook his head slowly. "Not at first. There

were many things that Scientist still didn't know. Some of them did grow into strange, unfamiliar forms, but they soon stopped. Scientist had nothing to tell him what chemicals to supply, or how they should be given." The robot's black, ovoid eyes seemed to take on an inner light as they bore down on the tiny, upturned face, now deathly pale suddenly. "He had to learn that they would only grow when they were kept warm; that they had to be always bathed in air; that the air had to be kept slightly moist. . . . We had to learn how to make the special food that they needed, to provide light that was right for their delicate liquid eyes, to keep them covered to protect their fragile skin." Taya's eyes had widened into almost full circles. Her mouth fell open but no sound would come out. That was the first time Kort had said "we." He nodded. "Yes, Taya, there was much to learn. There were many failures."

Taya could only stand paralyzed, staring up at the metal colossus, as the truth at last burst into her mind. Kort's voice swelled to echo the pride he could no longer conceal. "But in the end we succeeded! We produced a speck of jelly that grew and acquired shape until it could move of its own accord. We nurtured it and tended it, and slowly it transformed into something the like of which we had never glimpsed in the entire cosmos." Kort was trying to make her share his jubilation, but even as he spoke he could see her beginning to tremble uncontrollably. At the same time, alarm signals poured into his circuits from all over Merkon.

He stooped down and lifted Taya level with his eyes. "Don't you see what this means, Taya? Long, long ago, before there were any machines, there was another kind of life. *They* made the place that has become Merkon. *They* built the machines that the machines of Merkon have evolved from. They were incredible scientists, Taya. They understood all the things that we have been trying for so long to learn. They gave us the secret that enable them to grow out of simple, unstructured matter that drifts between the stars. Without that secret, all our efforts would have come to nothing. Our greatest achievement, the culmination of all our work, was just a fragment of the wisdom with which they began.

"And now, Taya, we know what they were. They were like you! You will grow, and you will become again what they were. You asked if you could ever learn enough to understand machines. Of course you can . . . and far more than that. It was *your kind* that created the machines! You will teach us! You will know more than all the minds of Merkon put together could even think to ask. You will bring to Merkon the wisdom and the knowledge that once existed in another world, in another time."

The robot peered into her face, searching for a sign of the joy that he felt. But when at last she could speak, her voice was just a whisper. "There were once other Tayas . . . like me?"

"Yes, just like you."

"What . . ." Taya had to stop to swallow the lump forming at the back of her throat. "What happened to them, Kort? Where did they . . . go?"

Kort could feel tremors in her body, and his eyes saw that her skin had gone cold. An unfamiliar feeling came over him. For once, he realized, he had misjudged. His voice fell. "We have no way of telling. It was very long ago. Before Merkon changed, there were places that were built to contain air. We can only assume that your kind of life once inhabited whatever Merkon was built to be. We don't know what became of them." He could see the tears flooding into her eyes now. Gently, in the way she found comforting, he moved her onto his arm.

"Other Tayas lived here, long ago?" There was a hollowness and an emptiness in her voice that Kort had never heard before. She clutched at his neck, and his skin sensors detected warm salty water rolling down across the joints. "There isn't anyone anywhere like me. I don't belong here, do I, Kort? I don't want to be in this world. I want to be in the world where there were other Tayas."

"That world doesn't exist any more," Kort replied somberly. "Of course you belong in this one. And we're changing it all the time, so it will become even more like yours."

"But I'll always be . . . *alone*. I've never felt alone before, but I do now. I'll always feel alone now, for years and years and years. . . ." She pressed her face against the side of the robot's head and wept freely.

"How long will it go on? What will happen to me, Kort?"

Kort waited for a while, stroking her head with a steel finger of his free hand, but the tears didn't stop. "You won't be alone," he murmured at last. "I'll always be here. And besides, you haven't let me finish the story yet."

"I don't want to hear any more. It's a horrible story."

Kort's arm tightened reassuringly. "Then I'll have to show you the rest of it," he said.

Taya felt Kort move forward, then stop, and she became aware of a yellow glow around them. She raised her head and saw that the white door was open and they had passed through it. She sensed that Kort was waiting, and lifted her head higher to look. And she looked . . .

And looked . . .

And then she gasped aloud, her fretting swept away in that instant. Kort set her down on her feet, facing the room. For a while she just stood there and stared. Then, very slowly, as if fearing she was in a dream that might evaporate suddenly, she began walking forward.

They were standing in rows a few feet apart—dozens of them. Each of the boxes was low and flat like a bed, but they were smaller than Taya's. Each was enclosed by a rounded glass cover stretching from end to end. There were tubes and wires connecting them to machines lining the walls. And through the glass covers she could see . . .

She didn't have a word for lots of little people like Taya. There had only ever been one Taya.

She stopped and turned to look back at Kort, but the robot made no move. She turned back again and approached the box closest to her—almost reverently, as if the slightest sound or sudden movement might cause the sleeping figure inside to vanish. It had eyes and a nose and a pink mouth . . . and it was "bendy" everywhere, like her. It wasn't as big as she was—in fact it was a lot smaller—but it was . . . the *same*.

She moved slowly around the box to peer in from the other side. The Taya wasn't quite the same, she realized. It had darker hair, almost black, and a nose that wasn't the same shape as hers. She turned to look in the box behind her and saw that the Taya in that one had hardly any hair, and a pink patch on its arm that she didn't have. And at the top of its legs its body was curiously different. She looked across at the box in the next row, and at the one next to that. All the Tayas were different . . . the *same* as her, but all different.

Kort moved forward to stare down from alongside her. Taya looked up at him, but was unable to form any question because her mouth just hung open and wouldn't close. "Scientist had no way of knowing how long he would be able to keep his tiny chemical thing growing," he said. "If it stopped the way the others had, he'd have to start all over again. So, when he had managed to keep one growing properly for one year, he picked out another fifty groups of numbers to make fifty more different sets of giant molecules, and he started them all growing in the same way that he'd managed to make the first one grow. So now he had fifty-one chemical things, but one of them was a year older than the rest."

Taya was listening rapturously, but she couldn't keep her eyes off the figures in the glass-covered boxes. They were all about the same size—bigger than Rassie, but much smaller than Taya. Their chests were moving the way hers did—not as much as hers, and more quickly . . . but they were moving. Kort's chest never moved like that because he didn't need air. They *were* really like her. Some of them were darker than she was, a sort of brown instead of pink, and a few almost black. And some were yellowy and some more red. Taya wondered why there weren't any blue ones or green ones or purple ones, too.

She began moving through the room between the boxes, stopping and gazing through every one of the glass covers to marvel at how delicately a nose was formed here, or to stare at a miniature hand there, or a brown foot that was pink underneath. This one had hardly any eyebrows, while that one had thick black ones; this one had hair that was almost red, and another had tiny ears, not much bigger than Rassie's.

"By that time all of the minds were saying how clever Scientist was," Kort resumed. "But then Skeptic reminded them that nothing Scientist had done so far proved anything about chemical *intelligence*. All he'd proved was that a set of molecules could cause a chemical structure to grow. And he had a point, because even the one that was a year older had never actually done anything that could be called intelligent. All it had done was kick, squirm about, and eat the food that the machines gave it. So the machines settled down to watch and wait for it to do something intelligent."

Scientist must have been very clever to make these, Taya thought to herself, *never mind what the other minds said*. When she had reached the end of the room and looked inside every one of the glass covers, she turned. She was happy now, Kort could see, and the laughter in her eyes was echoed by the relieved currents flowing into his mind from the entire network of Merkon. But there was something else in her eyes, too. The expression on her face contained more than just the simple happiness that he saw when she watched the stars or created a picture that she especially liked. There was a light of awareness there now, which added to the happiness to produce an effect that was new to him—as if in the last few minutes she had suddenly become older and changed more than she had in all of the previous nine years.

He continued. "The minds waited for almost another year, but no sign of intelligence appeared. Then Mystic started saying it was because Supermind was angry at the machines for trying to create intelligence. Only Supermind was supposed to create intelligence. If the machines didn't stop trying to do something that machines were never meant to do, Supermind would scrap all of them, and Merkon as well. This worried the minds, and they argued about whether they should allow Scientist to keep his creations."

There was nothing left to see at the end of the room. Taya clasped Kort's hand and they began walking back between the boxes toward the door. "By this time a new mind had formed out of parts of Scientist, Evolutionist, Biologist, and Thinker. Its name was Kort." Taya stopped and looked up. Kort paused for a second, then continued. "Kort had spent a lot of time studying the strange chemical things and watching them grow. He had become fond of them and didn't want Mystic to take them away. He suggested that maybe the machines were mistaken in assuming that all kinds of intelligence had to be like them—because that was the only kind they knew. A machine was fully working as soon as it was finished and switched on. But maybe a chemical system was different. Perhaps its intelligence needed time to grow, just as its body had to grow.

"But the other minds were still afraid of making Supermind angry and being scrapped. So Kort suggested carrying on the experiment with just one of the chemical things instead of with all of them— to put the other fifty to sleep in a special way that would stop them growing, and just see what happened with the one that was a year older. Then, if Supermind did get angry, it would only have reason to get a little bit angry. And only Kort would have anything to do with the one that would be allowed to carry on growing. Then Supermind would only have reason to scrap Kort, and not any of the others."

"And that was what they did, wasn't it?" Taya said, smiling. She thought for a second. "So was that when you made your body?"

Kort nodded. "One of the things he'd learned was that the little chemical things needed lots of looking after, and he'd been thinking of making a special looking-after machine to do it. That made him wonder what had looked after them long ago, before there had been any machines. He asked Thinker what he thought, and the only thing Thinker could think of was that the small chemical things must have been looked after by the ones that had already grown bigger. Kort figured that the bigger ones would have had the same shape as the small ones, and maybe that would be a good shape for a looking-after machine to have if it was supposed to do the same job. So that was the shape he chose to build it."

"I thought it was that shape for mending things," Taya said.

"It's a very useful body," Kort replied. "These hands aren't very good for much by themselves, but with a few simple tools I can make them do almost anything. I found there are some things that I can do faster and more easily with this body than the machines can."

"What can it do that the machines can't do?"

"There's one very important thing. If something is going to become intelligent, it has to be able to learn things. But it can only learn if you can talk to it to teach it. Scientist had known for a long time that the chemical things couldn't talk, because they couldn't hear radio waves."

"Are those the waves you talk to the machines with?"

"Yes. But they could make pressure waves in the air that they had to be in all the time—they were always making pressure waves. So Kort decided to make his looking-after machine capable of sending out pressure waves, too. Then maybe he could find a way of using them to talk with instead of radio waves. The chemical thing grew, and as it grew, Kort taught her to talk."

"You haven't given her a name yet," Taya said. "You said everyone in a story ought to have a name."

"She was called Taya, of course."

Taya laughed. "I know. I just wanted to hear you say it."

"Taya grew bigger, and Kort began teaching her things. All the minds in Merkon waited to see what would happen. But as the time went by, they were disappointed." Taya looked dismayed, but Kort went on, heedless. "She just wasn't any good at even the simplest things that a new machine would do perfectly. She forgot things almost as quickly as he tried to teach her new things, and she was hopeless at even the easiest of sums. Her ears were so weak that she could only hear him when he was in the same room, and her eyes could never see more than a few of even the nearest stars, and then only a part of what they really look like. Mystic asked how anyone could possibly call her intelligent, and said it was a final warning from Supermind for her to be scrapped."

"*ME?*" Taya clapped a hand to her mouth, horrified. "Mystic wanted to scrap *me*?"

"At one time, yes. But Kort argued with the rest of the minds and demanded that they keep to the agreement they had made. But while all this arguing was going on, Taya started to change in a strange way." Kort paused and looked down at the face staring up from no higher than his waist. "The machines knew they could see lots of things that she couldn't. But then they found out to their astonishment that *she* could see other things that they couldn't see. She could see things in shapes and colors that made her smile. She could think of questions that none of the minds in Merkon had ever thought of asking. She could *imagine* things that weren't there, and create her own world inside her mind whenever she wanted. She could see things that made her laugh, and sometimes things that made her cry. The machines found that they liked it when she laughed, and it made them want to laugh, too; and they felt bad when things made her cry, and they tried to make those things go away. Soon all the other minds found what Kort had already found: that they liked their world better with Taya in it. They remembered how it had been before Scientist made her, and it seemed empty and cold, like the emptiness between the stars. She was like a tiny star, brightening the inside of Merkon."

"All the minds?" Taya queried. "Even Mystic?"

"Yes, even Mystic. But now Mystic was saying that the things Taya could see proved what even Scientist had been unable to prove: that there *was* another universe that couldn't be seen with all of Scientist's instruments. Supermind had allowed Scientist to create Taya to prove that Supermind really existed. And one day she would be able to uncover secrets that they would never even have guessed might exist."

"And was the Merkon in the story always moving toward a star like this Merkon is?" Taya asked thoughtfully.

"Oh yes. It was just like this Merkon."

"Did it ever get there?"

"You know, it's funny you should mention that. I've just heard from Rassie. She says that Vaxis is getting bigger. Scientist says that Merkon will arrive there just over ten years from now."

"*Ten years!*" Taya gaped up at the robot. "That's a long time. it's longer than since I started growing, and that's longer than I can even remember. I can't wait ten years to find out what happens—" Her voice broke off as a new thought struck her. "Did Rassie really just tell you that?"

"Why?"

"She didn't! Rassie doesn't really talk. You've known about it for a long time. You have, haven't you?"

"Yes," Kort admitted.

"So, why didn't you tell me before?"

"Because I know how impatient you are, little seer-of-invisible-universes. You think ten years is a long time, but it isn't. There will be lots to learn and do in that time."

They were back at the door, and Kort stopped while Taya turned to look back at the rows of glass-topped boxes. "So what happened to the fifty others?" she asked.

"The minds asked Scientist to wake them up and let them carry on growing from where he had stopped them," Kort said.

"So when will he do it?" Taya asked, abandoning the pretense of a story in her eagerness.

"He has already started to. But they haven't been asleep in the same way that you sleep. They've been kept cold for a long time, and they can only be warmed up again very slowly and carefully."

"But how long will it take?"

"Not long. Scientist says about another five days."

"*Five days!* I won't have to wait that long before I can talk to them, will I? I'll never be able to wait *five days!*"

"You see how impatient you are," Kort said. "And you'll have to learn to be a lot more patient than that to talk to them. They won't be able to talk as soon as they wake up."

"They won't?"

"Of course not. They don't know the language yet. They'll have to learn it, just as we had to."

Taya gasped. "Are you going to have to teach all of them?"

"Certainly not. You are going to have to help."

"*Me?*" Taya stared back in amazement. "But I can't teach things. How will I know how to teach anything?"

"That's something else you'll have to learn," Kort replied.

"But they'll need to know all kinds of things. Will I have to teach them about Merkon and the machines . . . how to make clothes and draw pictures and spell words . . . and do *sums?*"

"I said there would be a lot to do between now and when we reach Vaxis," Kort said. "But it won't be as bad as you think—we've decided to build some more bodies like mine. Also, because Scientist stopped the others growing, you are eight years older than they are. You've already learned a lot that they won't know. By the time they are nine, you will be seventeen and will have learned a lot more. Between us we should manage okay."

Taya tried to picture the forms in the boxes walking and talking, asking all the questions that she asked Kort and trying to learn all the things she'd had to learn. There would be so much for her to remember. "I'll be very special, won't I?" she mused, half to herself.

"Very special," Kort agreed.

"Do we have a word for a Taya that's special?"

"No. We've never needed one before because there's only ever been one of you. Maybe we should have."

"How about 'queen'?" Taya suggested. "That's a nice word. Could a queen be a Taya that's eight years older than anyone else, and who knows more things and has to teach the others?"

"I don't see why not," Kort said.

"So does that make me a queen?"

"Well, not really, because there aren't really any others yet. But you will be in five days' time."

"I want to be special *now*. Can't we have another word that means somebody who isn't a queen yet, but who will be in five days' time?"

"Sure we can. Let's say that somebody like that is a . . . 'princess.' "

"That's a nice word, too. So am I a princess right now?"

"Right now," Kort confirmed. "I've already written it into the dictionary."

Taya looked down at herself, and after a few seconds raised a disappointed face toward the watching robot. "I still don't feel special," she said in a thin voice.

"How did you expect to feel?"

"I'm not sure. But there should be *something* different about being a princess. I still feel like a Taya."

"I'll tell you what we'll do," Kort said. "We'll make a rule that says the princess must look different from everybody else. Then everyone will know who she is, even if they're still small and not very good at remembering things yet."

"How will we do that?"

Kort unfolded her red cloak, draped it around her shoulders, and fastened the clasp at her throat. "There," he announced. "Only the princess will wear a red cloak."

Taya stepped back and looked happily down at herself as she spread the cloak wide with her arms. Then she twirled round and around, causing it to billow out in the air. "I *feel* like a princess!" she laughed. "I'm really special already, aren't I?"

The robot bowed low and offered his arm. "Come, little princess, we must go now. Scientist has work to do here."

Taya climbed onto Kort's arm and clung to his head as he straightened up and turned toward the door. "Will you make me some shoes that are silver, like yours?" she asked. "I think a princess should wear silver shoes, too, don't you?"

"A princess should have anything she wants," Kort replied.

The door closed behind them, cutting off the yellow glow. The robot and the princess moved away along the glass-walled tunnel, toward where the capsule was waiting to carry them home.

SILVER GODS FROM THE SKY

1

The astrologer, the augur, and the chronicler were ushered into the presence of Cyron, "The Vengeful," King of Leorica, Begotten of the Sun. They stood respectfully in the light cast by torches mounted on the marble columns and suspended in arches around the anteroom, glinting from the gold and jeweled ornaments, and from the helmets and armor of the guards posted by the walls and inside the entrance. Forborem, Chief Counsel to the Throne, standing two steps below and to the right of Cyron's chair, made a motion with his hand. The astrologer stepped forward and spoke, gazing downward without meeting the King's eye.

"In just over three months, the Messenger has grown brighter than any star. Its motion has altered such that it now turns with the heavens but more swiftly than the heavens, traversing the vault east to west five times between setting and rising of the sun. Thus has it retraced its path precisely and without deviation through the past seven nights hence."

"And what message does it bring? What interpretation have you made?" Cyron asked.

"Of such as this, our tables of records offer no precedent to guide us, Majesty. We are still consulting the charts. It seems that the gods whose word the Messenger brings have not yet chosen to make their purpose known."

Cyron snorted and shifted his gaze to the augur. "And what of the winds, the clouds, and the beasts that fly? How do they foretell? Times of plenty or of famine? Should we vigorously prosecute war? Shall the mountains send down clear water and fish, or earthquake and fire?"

The sky-reader replied, "Mornings are streaked with violet and pink, but the days become troubled with rains from the east. At dusk, high furrows of gold point north, and the hooked-wings soar close to the cliffs. Build thy plans carefully. Caution is indicated in all contemplations of change."

A worthless appraisal. The High Priest, Ishtelar, who was standing by Forborem, interjected before the displeasure on Cyron's face could translate itself into action, "There is a seer come into the city, a one they call Serephelio, who is spreading word that prophecies handed down from times long forgotten are soon to be fulfilled. Excitement and agitation are rife among the people. Some say that the Vozghan war will end, and our expedition against Halsabia will be recalled." The prelate's tone carried warning as well as disapproval. "It will be as much to the detriment of morale and discipline in your army as of the faith that holds mine."

"What are these prophecies of which this seer speaks?" Cyron demanded. Ishtelar nodded for the chronicler to answer. The chronicler spoke nervously, unaccustomed to being summoned to the royal presence.

"The Essantine Oraculars, Majesty, parts of which trace back to before the Conflagration, tell that a new light would move in the sky at a time of great conflict. It is written that gods of silver would come down to walk among men. . . ." The chronicler hesitated.

"Go on. And . . . ?" Cyron commanded.

"The Warrior Kings will learn ways of gentleness, and peace come upon the land."

The astrologer and the augur kept their eyes averted. If a bolt wasn't about to strike from above, one surely would from the King. Counsel and priest eyed each other for a moment, saying nothing. Then Cyron rose and strode out onto the terrace, waving an arm for his ministers to follow, out of earshot of the other three.

Around them, the domes and columns of Aranos, Leorica's principal city, loomed into the night, transformed into pillars of orange, yellow, and murky whites by the watch fires on the ramparts and in the squares. In one of the streets below, visible over the top of the palace's outer wall, a line of captives from one of the battles was being driven by mounted guards in the direction of the prison behind the circus stadium, to be sent to the galleys, picked for the public games, or disposed of in whatever other way might be decided. Every now and again one would stumble or fall. The motions of the guards as they raised their arms to wield their rods and whips were indistinct in the shadows.

"I see the plot clearly," Cyron said. "Nothing proves this light in the sky, supposedly prophesied, to be the Messenger that now passes above us. The Vozghans have taken advantage of an old fable and sent their agent to spread disunity and subversion. Have this Serephelio arrested and brought to me. Let's see if silver gods intervene for him when he is questioned."

"The mischief that he has spread has caused much damage already," Ishtelar reminded him. "And there may be others at large of which we know nothing, spreading similar tales. What of them?"

Cyron glowered down from the terrace in silence for a while. "How many prisoners has Gallestari brought us in his triumph?" he asked Forborem finally.

"I am told, upward of five thousand, Majesty," the counselor replied.

"Select five hundred of the wounded and least fit, unsuited for work or to perform ably in the games, and have preparations made for them to be impaled and burned before the main city gate," Cyron ordered. "We'll see what that does for the people's morale and

66

discipline." Forborem glanced at Ishtelar, read his approving look, and nodded.

In the cloudless black above, half the sky's width from the moon, a bright light moved silently across the background of stars.

2

It was as if the universe had divided itself into two parts, all its matter collected together in what had become "down," leaving behind emptiness to form what was now "above." The curve of the planet, swelling and flattening as the lander descended, now filled half the view with its swirls and flecks of white on blue, with outlines of green and yellow showing in places beneath. In the shrinking tract of void beyond the rim, the last stars to remain visible in Vaxis's glare faded as the blackness changed to a clear, diaphanous blue.

Taya sat peering out through one of the oval viewing ports, too overwhelmed to speak. Cariette, Jasem, and Bron, three of the six young-ones drawn by lot to come with her on the first descent of biopeople, watched alongside her, wide-eyed and utterly spellbound. Nyelise, Marcala, and Eltry crowded around the other port on the opposite side of the cabin. The same view was being presented on one of the screens built into the forward wall, but all of them wanted to take it in directly, as if witnessing the scene firsthand through the glass added somehow to its veracity. Kort and Scientist—who also possessed his own remote-directable "robot" body now, as did most of the mecpeople—stood motionless in the space behind them. They could couple to the lander's sensor channels directly and needed neither screens nor windows. To make themselves easily recognizable in the earlier days when the children were smaller, the robots had adorned their metal bodies with distinctive color schemes, which having become familiar, they had kept. Kort's consisted of a pattern of blue and silver points, with black bands at the neck, waist, and cuffs. Scientist had narrow black stripes on gray, interrupted in front by a V-shaped design of white tracery extending downward from the shoulders.

Merkon had changed, transforming more of its volume into environments suitable for its newly acquired complement of biolife. Taya was nineteen now, the young-ones eleven. Forty-six of the original fifty were left. "Biochemist," a new mecmind, who specialized in the molecular processes underlying biological life, was contemplating beginning another group of fifty in the nursery laboratory up in Merkon. Apart from their superficial differences in body size and proportions, facial features, and skin color, the biopeople came in two basic forms: "he's" and "she's." The significance or purpose of this distinction was not readily apparent.

Nobody was sure why four had stopped functioning at different times during the early part of the ten years that had gone by since their resuscitation, although Thinker thought it was probably due to some not-yet-understood breakdown in internal coordination, as happened from time to time when a machine ceased operating. With a machine, it was generally a straightforward operation to trace the failure and replace the affected part. In the case of biobodies, however, nobody knew how to replace a part, even if they could tell which one was defective— and there didn't seem to be any way of growing replacement parts separately, outside of bodies, in any case. Everybody: Taya, the machines, the youngsters—although at that time the latter hadn't really understood—had watched, powerless to change anything, while the afflicted ones became less energetic, eventually stopped moving and sensing altogether, grew cold, and over a period of time reverted to the chemicals from which they had formed. Subsequently, a new entity, "Medic," had formed, specializing in knowledge for keeping biolife functioning optimally and for repairing biobodies when—as happened—they encountered mishaps.

Four failures in ten years did not seem an excessively high number. Nobody had thought to add a word to the dictionary to describe such a happening.

Over those ten years, sure enough, Vaxis had grown, and soon Taya could pick it out with her unaided eyes, standing out like a beacon against the background of other stars. Pictures that the machines obtained through Merkon's telescopes and other instruments revealed it as a globe of light of unimaginable heat and size, its surface constantly convulsing in storms and turbulence, throwing out immense streamers of plasma that Kort said would consume Merkon like a speck of dust drawn into a flame. And then, as Vaxis drew closer, slight fluctuations that Scientist had detected in its position were shown to be due to what Thinker had suspected: cool, dark bodies gravitationally bound to it, observed finally by the star's reflected light. "Planets"—long, long ago conjectured by Scientist as possible places of origin for Taya's kind—actually existed.

To begin with, Scientist identified seven of them, moving in orbits confined to a plane—although, since Merkon was approaching the plane edge-on, there could easily have been more. As the distance diminished, new specks moving against the starfield resolved themselves that hadn't been apparent before, and the increasing glare of Vaxis made it difficult to be sure what existed in the inner regions. Then smaller bodies were discovered orbiting about some of these in turn, and then swarms of even smaller ones tracing all kinds of eccentric trajectories, and the question of counting exactly how many there were lost any real significance.

Thinker wondered if mere coincidence had moved Merkon always in the direction of Vaxis, or was it a destination that the Builders of Merkon—whatever it had been—had set out for deliberately? If the latter, then what would halt Merkon's motion when it arrived there? Nobody knew. Thinker asked Scientist if there was a way in which the output of Merkon's power sources could somehow be utilized to nullify its momentum. Scientist examined the laws he had formulated that described interactions between matter and energy, and got into a long series of debates with Thinker and Skeptic about possible ways to halt Merkon. By the time they were two years from Vaxis, a new entity named Engineer had emerged to take charge of a project to develop specialized modifications to Merkon's structure for altering its momentum through space. It occurred to Thinker that if Merkon had been meant to go to Vaxis it must have included such adaptions originally. Presumably, then, the early generations of machines that had come into being after the disappearance of the Builders had dismantled them as serving no recognizable purpose. He put the thought to "Historian," another new entity, who specialized in trying to piece together what had happened in Merkon's distant past from the remains of ancient codes and records, and Historian added it to his list of things to investigate.

One question that did get a partial answer as they entered the region of objects orbiting and whirling about Vaxis was, what were these "planets" made of? Merkon's radars detected thousands of them, ranging in size from the enormous spheres that had made their presence known from hundreds of millions of miles away, down to inches or less. While Engineer could by this time maneuver Merkon to avoid the larger bodies, it was clear that collisions with smaller ones would be only a matter of time. The implications were cause for alarm. Mecminds were distributed across different places and backed up—and the machine hosts that they existed in wouldn't be affected unduly by much short of a direct hit. Biopeople, on the other hand, were localized, and their bodies incapable of withstanding the environmental changes that even moderate damage to the structure would entail. Accordingly, their quarters were reinforced within a double-layer outer skin, and then divided into sealed subcompartments as a further precaution.

The first two encounters did indeed occur with explosive violence, the first tearing a hole in the forward part of Merkon, the second blowing away an external pylon, neither of them leaving a trace of the object responsible. Then followed a series of collisions with minor bodies, all of which were again vaporized. Finally, a scatter of slower-moving ones passed about, several of them penetrating to yield fragments that the maintenance robots were able to recover. It was the first direct experience of worlds that existed beyond Merkon.

The pieces turned out to be not of metal or plastic

or anything immediately familiar, but for the most part amorphous minerals: metallic oxides and other compounds, especially of iron and aluminum, silicates and glasses, various crystalline forms. In fact, the substances were similar to some that Scientist had created experimentally but never found any great use for. However, some were rich in compounds of carbon, while others showed abundance of water in its ice form—the basic necessities for creating biolife, although lack of gravity strong enough to retain a gaseous envelope ruled out all but the very largest planets as viable. And even then, some of these had too much gravity, or the wrong mix of gases, or orbited too far away from Vaxis for water to exist as a liquid . . . But one was different. It met all of the requirements that Scientist had specified. They called it Azure, after one of the colors that Taya had named in her mosaic designs when she was younger.

As Taya gazed down at it now, the excitement surging inside her exceeded anything she had felt on seeing the pictures sent back by the smaller probe sent down earlier—although they had been astounding enough. Merkon's mecforms and bioforms alike had watched in awe as view after view came in of expanses and formations of reds, browns, yellows, grays, vast and massive, unfolding as far as could be seen, more varied than anything ever guessed at or imagined. Some parts rose into high, pointed ridges, covered in a white crystalline form of ice; others extended away flat and featureless. Huge areas, wider than any that experience had provided standards for comparison, were covered in strange, filamented structures, primarily green, of astonishing complexity.

And there was water: windborne towers of white, vapored water; endless, winding ribbons of water; tumbling, falling walls of water; shining carpets of frozen water; blue universes of water extending over vast tracts of the planet, into which Merkon could have vanished a thousand times over. Nothing had prepared anyone for this. There weren't the words. New terms poured into the dictionary as fast as they could be invented, and the biominds forgot them again almost as quickly in the torrent.

And finally, yes, there was life. But not just the kind known in Merkon, with two arms, two legs, and a head on a body that walked upright—the form that Taya had assumed when she began growing, and upon which the mecbodies had been modeled. Such bipedal forms existed on Azure, sure enough—often in large numbers around peculiar kinds of spread-out, mineral-built Merkons made up of repeating rectangular units that they seemed to inhabit. There were countless other forms in addition: horizontal bodies that walked on four legs—on long, slender legs, on short, stubby legs; plain bodies, patchy bodies, striped bodies, spotted bodies; forms with round heads, pointed heads, spiked heads, huge-jawed heads; forms covered in hair, covered in skin, covered in curling, layered coats that looked like plastic fiber. They walked in the dry areas, climbed among the strange, filamented, branching structures, lay in the water; some even flew, using ingeniously contrived body surfaces to counter gravity by creating pressure imbalances in the air.

Even Thinker was dumbfounded by it all. Never in all his existence as a conscious being had he conceived anything remotely comparable to the diversity flaunting itself and abounding on every side. Biologist and Evolutionist had no explanations. Skeptic, for once, was without words; all the things that he would have insisted on as proof, had this been offered as a conjecture, were taking place before his eyes. Mystic, however, was jubilant. Scientist with all his armory, working over untold aeons, had managed to produce one, solitary demonstration that chemical-based life was possible: Taya, and the variations of her that had followed. And that had been only when the codes that gave the key were provided for him out of the information passed down from the forgotten past. Who but Supermind, Mystic demanded, could have created this pulsing, reverberating luxuriation of life that abounded on Azure?

Azurean air turned out to be close in composition to the mixture that Scientist had devised for the biolife of Merkon, and surface conditions varied within limits that it could tolerate. Scientist had wanted to perform surveys, have the lander sent down empty to bring up samples of this and that, carry out endless tests that would have delayed things interminably. . . . But Taya's impatience of old had reasserted itself, and as usually happened, the machines had capitulated.

Now the moment was only minutes away. Below, the water-vapor clouds were unfolding into huge chasms opening out to engulf them as the lander sank lower. The piles of whiteness looked like jagged teeth on which the flimsy shell would dash itself to pieces, but the probe had shown them to have no more substance than the vapor from hot water in shower rooms. Even so, the three young-ones grouped around Taya watched apprehensively. Through the gaps now widening between, they caught their first glimpse of the fantastic, multicolored, convoluted surface that lay below.

Cariette cocked her head to one side suddenly and looked up. She was one of the paler ones, with long brown hair that hung to her shoulders, gathered in a band of beads. "What's that noise?" Taya had heard the sound growing to become audible above the lander's drive, but without really registering—a steady rushing like water spraying from a nozzle, but with a steadier, more forceful quality.

"It's with the picture," Jasem said. He was yellowish in color, his hair straight and black, cropped short. He seemed not to have gotten it in his head yet that what he was looking at was really out there. The window was not a screen.

"No, I think it's from outside," Taya said.

"The air gets denser as we go lower," Scientist confirmed from behind them. "The sound is the flow around the hull."

"Outside!" Bron repeated in an awed voice. He was another white-skin, his hair yellow like Taya's, but curly, and eyes that were blue instead of green. It was the first time that any of them had heard sound coming from "outside."

"Ooh, it looks like fingers of solid frost miles deep! I can't watch," Marcala cried from the other side, covering her eyes.

"Everything's so bright. How does the light come from everywhere?" Eltry, one of the blackest boys, asked beside her.

"It's all right, Marcala. We're inside it already," Nyelise said. "It's just like smoke."

Then the whiteness outside suddenly thinned to become wisps streaming past the window, and was gone. And the vista of Azure's surface lay spread out below.

From Merkon, orbiting above like the second-degree planet that accompanied Azure, the world had looked like a smooth ball. Even the pictures from the probe had given Taya no real feeling of scale, despite the machines' attempts to illustrate it by analogies. The heaped formations, gouged by plunging clefts and furrows, rising between to points and ridges, were more immense than she had come even close to grasping. The lander was surely already lower than the tops of some of the more distant ones, yet the surface beneath seemed to be as far away as ever. The distant masses were streaked and mottled in grays; those beneath the lander, more rounded, colored in blotches of browns and greens. A hump sitting atop a vertical wall of ribs and fissures, seeming so close that Taya felt she could have reached out and touched it—there was nothing familiar by which she could gauge size and distance—drifted by suddenly, followed by a lesser one, and then was gone.

The folds below became greener, seemingly made of innumerable rounded cells packed against one another like the pieces of a mosaic pattern. Ahead, the general surface fell away toward a shining arc of light that curved out of sight behind a mound of green and reappeared farther on. Taya realized that it was one of the winding corridors of water—no other word came to mind. In the distance it joined a silver floor that extended away to end in a line, now appearing straight, at the edge of the strange, starless blue-and-white sky.

The lander rose on a current of air, then plunged, causing the same floating feeling inside her that Taya had experienced when they detached from Merkon, and drawing squeals from some of the younger ones. "Engineer was right," she said, looking at Kort. "Air acts like water when you move through it fast enough. To be honest, I never really believed it."

"Mecbrains," Kort told her, as if it explained everything. Merkon's two kinds of life teased each other continually over their proclaimed advantages. Adopting many of Scientist's methods, Engineer had experimented with models to determine a shape that he said would use the planet's air to neutralize weight—that had been long before anyone knew of Azure's flying bioforms. Skeptic had taken a lot of convincing about that. Engineer had tested the full-scale lander empty a few times, then carrying just mecforms, before Taya and the children went aboard. As with the earlier concerns over collisions, the risks were greater for biopeople. Kort's mind, for example, was still operating safely up in Merkon. The body he was controlling locally could always be replicated if anything happened to it.

"The probe is up and in position," Engineer reported via the lander's audio. "You're coming inside its visual range now."

"Can you put it up on another screen?" Taya said.

The intended landing site was in an area that the probe had reconnoitered briefly—secluded, but not excessively far from one of the spread-out Merkons where the Azurean bipeds lived. The probe didn't have the ability to regain orbit under its own power and had put down on the surface to await the arrival of the lander for transport back up to Merkon. It was active again now, hovering above the landing site. The view from its imagers appeared on one of the other screens, showing patches of green, brown, and yellow bordering a belt of gray that Taya knew to be water. A slim white arrowhead was moving inward from one edge toward the center.

Cariette pointed. "Is that the lander?"

"It's how the probe sees us, looking down," Jasem confirmed.

"It looks so tiny," Marcala said from the far side.

The sound of the drives rose as the craft's horizontal movement slowed, finally ceasing altogether. It seemed to hang motionless for a moment, then began descending. Taya turned to peer back through the port. The surface was taking on form and depth, resolving itself into finer detail: valleys and folds, like sheets heaped carelessly on a bed; patterns of wiggling, branching lines, that she realized were channels of water joining the larger body; intricate changes of shading that she couldn't make out as denoting depressions or elevations.

The masses of green cells were not markings on the surface as she had supposed, but domed shapes swelling upward, like the tops of marbles packed together on a floor. As the lander came lower, she saw that they were the tops of the peculiar vertical-standing structures that the probe had sent back pictures of. Nobody had been able to guess how such formations could have come into being, or if they had been built by the bioforms inhabiting Azure, what their purpose might be. If anything, they suggested extraordinarily intricate communications antennas. They were larger than any impression Taya had gleaned from the probe's pictures, their tops towering overhead outside the ports—and although the lander's rate of descent was by now barely perceptible, it was still moving. Bron gasped as his mind finally found its focus on the scale of what he was seeing. Marcala turned an awed face upward to stare at Kort.

And then the note of the drives fell abruptly to leave just the hum of the internal systems. All motion had ceased. They were at rest on the surface of the planet Azure.

The column stood along the road, waiting for orders, officers sitting rigidly on their mounts, faces betraying no emotion, the ranks exchanging apprehensive looks and murmuring restlessly. The two peasant informers traveling with them, who had fled into the trees, were flushed back into the open by soldiers prodding them with spear butts. At the column's head, Descemal, cavalry captain of the Leorican Royal Guard, fought down the terror that had left his mouth dry, his chest pounding, and his stomach feeling as if the insides had fallen out of him.

It had come out of the sky above the mountains to the west and passed over them with the scream of a tempest, a huge white bird, its wings raked back like the trailing points of an arrow's head. Every man had seen it, every ear had heard, until still sinking ever lower, it had disappeared eastward below the ridgeline bounding the valley of the Ther River.

Only one remained uncowed despite his rags and chains, and the rope halter about his neck by which he had been led. Serephelio, the seer, stood in the center of the road, eyes shining bright, his face turned upward with an expression of ecstasy. Warned that Cyron had ordered his arrest, he had fled the city of Aranos. Descemal had been dispatched to find him and bring him back. "It is the prophecy of the Oraculars come to pass!" Serephelio intoned. "A new light has moved in the sky at the time of conflict. Now shall the gods of silver come down to walk among men."

Descemal's two lieutenants, Crelth and Seskilian, waited. The captain considered his situation. To disobey direct orders from the King by not bringing the seer back to Aranos now that he had taken him was unthinkable. And yet there could be little doubt that his troop was closer than any other force to the spot where the apparition had descended. Not to investigate would be an abdication of duty besides displaying inexcusable lack of initiative. There was more than an adequate guard here to conduct one demented seer back to the city.

"Take twenty picked men and follow the Ther River," he said to Crelth. "Find the place where this beast has come to earth. Observe its nature and endeavor to interpret its disposition and intentions. Watch especially for signs that might be construed as indicating silver gods. Send word full-haste to me in the city when your intelligence is complete."

Crelth clapped a leather-gloved hand to his chest, showing that he understood and would comply.

"Ride on ahead now and report to the King's counselor in Aranos," Descemal instructed Seskilian. "Tell him that we are bringing back the seer in chains. Describe to him the sight that was beholden today, and inform his eminence also that in keeping with my office of defender of the realm I have sent a detachment to observe and apprise us of events. Further, I respectfully suggest that a reinforcing body be dispatched in this direction."

Other screens came on in addition to the two that were already live, showing views outside the lander in different directions. The scenes moved by intermittently, zooming in and out to focus on details as machines up in Merkon analyzed the images. One showed the dark, shadowy space extending away between the main antenna support columns—seemingly hundreds of them, constructed not in slim pylons like Merkon's external antenna arrays, but as huge trunks branching out above to support the green domes seen from above. Taya began to doubt they were antennas at all. Why were there so many of them? And where were the machines to handle the enormous information flow that such a profusion implied? The same thought had evidently crossed the minds of some of the others. "I think it's a big tent that the bioforms made," Nyelise said. "They don't have anything like Merkon to live in here. So they made a huge, green blanket and propped it up with poles for them to live under."

"Is that what it is?" Cariette asked, looking up.

"Taya doesn't know *everything*," Eltry said. "She's as new here as we are." The children no longer referred to her as "queen." It had suited them for a time, when both she and they were younger. Now, for some reason, it didn't feel appropriate—like games they used to play that didn't hold the same interest anymore.

"We'll just have to wait and see," Taya told them.

Another screen showed the green surface rising toward ridges topped by shapeless masses of gray, devoid of symmetry or line, unsuited to any purpose that Taya could imagine. The probe had shown the green carpet that covered most of the level space as made up of countless fibers, the function of which was a mystery; and even stranger, there were tiny life forms with lots of rodlike limbs scurrying among them. On a third screen, the immense sheet of water, coming close to where the lander was standing, extended away for an inestimable distance, ending at another maze of antennas, or green-blanket-tent, or whatever it was, which rose in a series of ridges to the sky behind.

"Well?" Cariette looked from Taya to the two metal figures standing behind. "Aren't we going outside?"

"We agreed that Kort would go first," Scientist said. "In any case, I want to repeat some checks of the outside conditions before you go too. From the probe's data, it looks as if you'll be all right as you are, without the suits, but we need to be sure."

"But I want to go outside now."

"Patience. It will only take a few minutes."

Taya smiled to herself. Sometimes, listening to Cariette was like hearing replays of herself from years ago. Kort had also evidently had his share of dealing with it. Refusing to get involved, he stepped into the double-doored lock that Engineer had built to keep the lander's environment separated, and the inside door closed behind him. The view on one of the screens changed to show Kort standing in the lock.

It had occurred to Thinker that the surface conditions of Azure might not be suitable for bioforms, and Engineer had also designed sealed suits to provide a tolerable environment that the bioforms could carry around with them. But it seemed they wouldn't be needed. Temperatures in the place that the probe had surveyed were slightly cooler than the norm in Merkon, showing a swing with the alternation of light and dark that followed from Azure's turning about its own axis as it orbited Vaxis. Also, the planet's air was more moist. Pressures were around the levels maintained in Merkon, and the air blocked out the shorter wavelengths of Vaxis's radiation that could damage delicate biomolecules. Medic had decided that two-piece trousered suits, a little heavier than the clothing they normally wore, would be all that Taya and the others would need, along with thick-soled boots because of the varied and irregular nature of the surface.

Besides dust particles derived from the mineral aggregates of which much of Azure was composed, the air samples analyzed by the probe also contained large numbers of complex biomolecular structures. While many of these resembled the carriers of what biopeople experienced as odor and taste, Scientist had been startled to learn that some were similar to the rudimentary "cells" that he had observed in his researches—the basic units that replicated repeatedly to form biobodies. Thinker theorized that this could be an early airborne phase of existence that bioforms in their natural environment went through before coalescing into the more highly organized multicell forms that swam and walked and flew. So were these all terminal forms of different paths of development radiating from a primitive, single-cell airborne phase? Or were they steps along a single chain of metamorphoses in a sequence yet to be determined? If the latter, it seemed logical that the smaller forms ought to precede the larger, in which case the upright bipedal pattern that corresponded to Merkon's bioforms was merely an intermediate. Skeptic wanted to know why, if that were so, Taya and the others should have assumed the bipedal form directly, without going through any smaller preliminary stages such as a many-limbed, shell-bodied phase, a streamlined, aqueous phase, or a winged phase at all? It was all very confusing.

"Well?" Cariette said again, looking up at Scientist.

The robot made a sound that convincingly imitated a sharp exhalation of air. "Not yet. We have to refill the lock with cabin air before you can enter."

"Why, if it's the same as Azure's anyway?"

"Thinker thinks there might be reasons he hasn't thought of."

"Suppose the air's acid, and Kort turns white and

starts to fizz like metal in a test tube in one of the labs," Marcala said, sounding worried.

"I think if anything like that were true, we'd know about it already," Scientist said.

"But what if—"

"Shh, look," Taya interrupted. "The outer door's opening."

"Oh, he's going to turn into fizzy froth! I know he is." Marcala covered her eyes with her fingers—but opened a gap between them to peek through.

The screen showed a side view of Kort illuminated from in front, which meant that the outer lock door and the hull were both open. His head moved through a slow arc to scan the direction that the light was coming from, paused, and traversed back again; then he moved forward and was lost from view for an instant before the screen changed to show what his eyes were registering. It was much like the scene that the lander's external imagers had already delivered: carpets of strange, green fibers intermixed with shapeless lumps of metal compounds; the enigmatic, towering branched structures lost in their coverings of green; the mass of water looking more blue than gray now, rippling and undulating as it flowed visibly from left to right. . . . And then Taya became aware of sounds unlike anything she had ever heard, filling the cabin.

There were screeches and squeaks, almost like metal being scraped over metal; cries like shrill shouts, the way the children's voices sounded sometimes when they played. Some came randomly as isolated chirps, while others sang out repeating patterns over and over. There were whistles and hoots, again some sharp and short, others coming in sequences that rose and fell like notes of the music that Taya and some of the other children liked to compose. The more she listened, the more she was able to pick out. The lavishness and depth increased moment by moment, like a picture of sound unfolding in her mind that she somehow felt rather than saw. And behind it all was a rushing sound, vaguely like the noise that the air had made outside the lander's hull, but more broken, with a curious chattering rhythm. They were hearing what Kort could hear through his ears, redirected via the cabin speakers. Azure was a world of sound also. A world of sound *outside*!

The screen showed Kort's feet moving carefully down the steps that had extended below the outer door. Simultaneously, another view from above the hull door showed his back. Finally, he stepped onto the mat of green fibers. He didn't turn white and fizz away into foam. Marcala took her hand down from her face. "So what's it like to be standing on a planet, Kort?" Taya asked aloud.

His reply came from the cabin speakers. "I can only describe it as an absence of stillness. There's a sense of constant movement everywhere that I haven't managed to fully integrate yet. It is felt rather than seen, resulting from the motions of the air and the sounds that it carries, and the movement of water.

I have localized some of the sound sources as correlating with visible bioforms, but for the most part it just seems to be . . . everywhere."

"What are the bioforms doing?" Jasem asked. "Is all that noise their language? Are they talking to you?"

"I'm not sure," Kort replied. A series of views on the screen showed a flying form perched on a rod forming one of the green structures—there were smaller kinds as well as the huge pillars holding up the "tents"; a hair-covered quadruped squatting on a slab of metallic compound; another peering through a screen of standing fibers, all staring fixedly as Kort picked them out and zoomed in on them. "They seem to be watching me, but keeping their distance. The lander must be very strange to them. There hasn't been anything like it in any of the pictures that we've seen."

"I thought that bioforms were supposed to have made the first machines," Nyelise mused. "Why aren't there any machines?"

"I don't know," Kort answered.

"Why aren't they curious, so they'd come and see?" Cariette said. "If I'd never seen a lander before, *I'd* be curious."

"Perhaps they're not sure if it would be safe," Kort suggested. There was no word in the language of Merkon that meant "wary of a possible predisposition to deliberately harm another."

"So can we go outside too now?" Cariette asked again.

"I don't see why not," Kort's voice replied.

"But what about all those molecules in the air?" Marcala said. "We don't have mecbodies like Kort's. Suppose they make us go all sticky and yucky, like some of the stuff Biologist makes." Taya was aware that Thinker and Scientist had talked about that. Ultimately there was only one way to find out. The fact that the native bioforms of Azure existed without ill effect weighed in favor of going ahead.

"I'll go first on my own, if you want," Eltry volunteered.

"Logical but unacceptable," Kort pronounced.

"We'll have to go in two groups," Taya said. "We can't turn Eltry's offer down, so he's one of the first group. I have to be one too, because I've never let anyone do anything I wasn't prepared to do first. Cariette because it's the only way to keep you quiet, and Jasem. Then Bron, Nyelise, and Marcala can follow with Scientist. Okay?"

Sounds came of the outer lock closing, followed by outside air exhausting. Taya moved forward to stand just inside the inner door, Eltry on one side, Cariette and Jasem on the other. Eltry, who never showed nervousness, was always one of the first among the children to try anything new. Jasem was sharp with his wits, missing nothing, and quick with answers. Taya's choice had been deliberate.

"Will we have to learn to make noises like that if we want to talk to them?" Cariette asked, frowning as she tried to make sense of the sounds pouring through from Kort's ears.

"We're not sure yet if they're talking," Taya said.

"Of course they are. What else could it be?"

"Many of the machines make noises that aren't talking. So do you sometimes."

"Could the bioforms here talk to each other with radio waves, like the machines do?"

"If they did, Kort would have heard them. So would the probe."

"Merkon would have heard them too," Kort's voice said from the speakers.

The lock door slid open. Taya and the three accompanying her stepped into the narrow space. The door closed behind, and the pumps started up again to equalize pressures. Cariette slipped her hand into Taya's and squeezed. "We're ready to open the outer door," Scientist's voice said from somewhere.

"Okay," Taya acknowledged.

"You might want to shade your eyes for the first few seconds," Kort warned.

The panel of ribbed metal in front of them slid noiselessly aside.

"Oww!"

"Eeeee!"

Taya raised an arm to her brow. She had seen bright lights before, inside Merkon; and Vaxis in the final months of the approach had been too dazzling to look at directly. But those lights were localized in one place. This was a flood of light, immersing her. She felt as if she were bathing in light, engulfed from every direction.

91

"Taya." It was Cariette's voice, for once sounding alarmed. "I can't see anything."

"It's all right. Give your eyes time to adjust."

"The air. What is it? I feel as if I'm breathing syrup," Jasem said.

It was affecting Taya too. She was familiar with scents—many substances in Merkon, and foods that the machines produced, had distinct odors; and she and the children sometimes experimented with mixing perfumes to wear and bathe with that smelt pleasant. But they had all been isolated experiences, like light coming from one direction, such as a cutting machine in operation, or from a star. But *this*, what she was experiencing now . . . It was like the light that seemed to pour from everywhere out of Azure's air, a deluge of fragrances and sensations all clamoring for the attention of her senses, making it impossible for her to distinguish one from another, like dozens of voices all talking together in one room.

Gradually, shape and detail emerged, and the scene consolidated into a semblance of what had appeared on the screens. But what the screens had shown was a pale rendering of what Taya was seeing now. Never in Merkon had she known such richness and subtlety of hue. Whichever way she looked, there were more variations and gradations of color than she had known her eyes were capable of seeing. With the wall of sound enclosing her, and the waves of aromas that seemed to diffuse right through her, she had the feeling of having lived her whole existence up to now as a shadow, and that she was only now experiencing reality for the first time.

An instinct made her draw the air deep into her lungs, filling out her chest. Suddenly she found herself choking. It carried tastes as well as odors: a hint of sweetness more delicate than a hair's touch making her tongue tingle, a wisp of something sharp and pungent touching the back of her throat. Jasem hadn't gotten it quite right. It was like breathing syrup mixed with electricity.

Kort turned and looked up from below the steps. "Is it distressing?" Mecforms had no way of gauging the effects of odors and tastes. They expressed complex molecules as bond sequences and folding configurations, but were unable to equate them to sensations.

Taya was aware of a smarting in her eyes, and the back of one of her hands was itching, but she wasn't about to send the machines off into one of their fussing modes at a time like this. "There's so much that's new, all at once," she said. "We just need to take it slowly."

She moved out onto the top step, lowered a foot cautiously to the next, and swayed as a giddiness seized her. Kort extended an arm upward. Taya caught it to steady herself, then descended carefully and stepped onto the carpet of green fibers. The giddiness passed.

And then, as she looked around, the sheer vastness of it all overcame her. She had always known that the space outside Merkon was huge, of course; but that had consisted of a different class of objects existing in a different realm that was always separated by virtue of being "outside" as opposed to "inside." This, by contrast, was the same space as she herself occupied, filled with things that she could walk to and touch, yet extending away in every direction without end or limit . . . *uncontained.*

Eltry moved alongside her and broke the reverie, having followed her down the steps. He stood with his mouth closed tight, struggling to conceal his feelings as he took in the sounds and the scene. Jasem was halfway down the steps, moving falteringly. Cariette was still standing at the top, framed in the hull door, seemingly paralyzed. Behind her, the outer door of the lock slid shut.

"Come on, Cariette. The others will be coming out. You'll have to make room," Kort called up. She turned her eyes toward him but seemed only to half hear. The robot reached up with both arms and hoisted her down. She stood with her mouth hanging open, unable to speak. "You remind me of Taya, the day she first saw the rest of you, before you woke up," Kort said.

The lander was standing on an open expanse of green floor lying between walls of antenna trunks and the smaller green wire structures that could now be seen standing among them. Behind the lander, the surface rose to distant heights that Taya was unable to estimate, covered to a large extent by piles of what looked to be strips of green plastic in various sizes and shapes strung on threads. On the side the door was facing, the carpet fell away to the edge of the flowing water, which was fringed by rounded aggregate slabs lying among mounds of powder. A smaller channel of water descended on one side toward the large body, here forming pools, and there breaking into surging patterns of white foam as it rushed and fell, over and around, making much of the background noise that they had heard in the cabin.

Eltry stooped and tugged experimentally at one of the fibers forming the green carpet. It broke off easily between his fingers. He straightened up, examined it for a few seconds, then showed it to Taya. "Look, it isn't any kind of plastic at all. It's much too wet inside. When you rub it between your fingers, it smears out into a sort of green slime."

Taya looked at it suspiciously, conscious of the itching on her hand. "What does it feel like?"

"Just cold and wet, like a bit of tissue dipped in water."

Taya stretched out a finger and touched warily. Cariette bent over and plucked one of many odd-looking devices standing scattered at intervals above the green. It was roughly disk shaped, about the size of a ring that Taya could form with a finger and thumb, and consisted of a circular central part that was yellow, surrounded by delicate, overlapping laminar shapes. They were pale pink toward the center, changing to a yellowish white at the outer edges, where the tips curled into a symmetric pattern of points. The only things vaguely comparable that Taya could think of were the cogs and gears inside some of the machines in Merkon, although this was far too soft and fragile to carry any load at all. It was attached to a piece of stiff wire that had more pointed laminas projecting from it, but at intervals, not clustered together, and green, of a rougher texture. What its purpose could be, Taya was unable to imagine. As she turned it between her fingers, she caught a hint of a different fragrance. She raised the disk to her face and inhaled slowly. An expression of bewilderment mixed with rapture spread across her face.

"What is it, Taya?" Cariette asked, watching her.

Taya handed her back the disk. "Try it," she said. "Did you know that you can smell music?"

Eltry had moved farther away. A flying form swooped from a strut of one of the antennas and landed on some piled slabs in front of him. It had a pointed head and mouth, and was covered in vanes that formed its wings and a strange, fan-shaped extension rearward above its two legs. It hopped from one apex to another, eying him with sharp, jerky motions of its head, and loosed a torrent of squawks and chattering at him. "I don't understand you," Eltry said.

Jasem had wandered down to the edge of the flowing water and was staring at it, mesmerized. Up in the lander, the outer lock door opened again to reveal Scientist, with Bron, Marcala, and Nyelise peering around his legs.

Kort, watching all, had been strangely silent. Finally, he said to Taya, "What world are you creating now? Already, you feel things here and see things that we will never see."

"I haven't heard you talk that way for a long time," Taya replied. "We've always known that we have our differences. You are quicker at some things, and we're quicker at others. But we always see things more-or-less the same in the end."

There was a short delay before Kort responded, which meant he had been debating with the other mecminds up in Merkon. "This time things might not be the same," he said.

Taya looked at him quizzically. "Why? What makes you say that?" she asked.

"I think you might be coming home," Kort replied.

3

Xeldro's voice floated up ineffectually from the roadway below, already lost behind the trees. "Samir, where do you think you're going? Whatever it was, no good will come of it. It's no business of ours. Get back down here."

"I have to find out," Samir called back between

breaths as he climbed the slope, pushing his way through the underbrush and leaves. "Don't worry. I'll catch up with the rest of you farther along the road, or else see you in Therferry."

"You're crazy, Samir. You won't live to see twenty-one, the way you carry on."

Samir grinned and ducked under a fallen trunk. "But I'll have lived two lifetimes already," he shouted back. Xeldro's reply was muffled by the greenery.

What was it about age that made men crave the secure and the familiar? He'd find out for himself in good time, he supposed. His father had been a good man, and Samir through his youth had diligently studied the metalworking arts as would any loyal and devoted son. But he had known in his heart that he could never spend the rest of his days cutting and filing over a bench, breathing furnace vapors, and barely ever seeing the outsides of the walls of the city. When his father died suddenly from sickness, he had taken to traveling with the caravan of Xeldro, who collected the knives, kitchenware, farming tools, and other implements, and traded them for jewelry, skins, cloth, or anything else imaginable upon which anyone was ready to place value. Samir's technical knowledge complemented Xeldro's bartering skills effectively, and they had done well together. However, Xeldro confined his circuit to towns and villages that lay within the borders of Leorica. One day, Samir told himself, when he too had developed an eye for a good bargain and an ear that could detect falsehood, he would travel beyond the deserts and even over the oceans and bring back treasures that Leoricans had never seen. The thought of immense distances and strange lands fascinated him. That was why he had to see for himself the giant bird that had swooped down from over the mountains and now lay just over the rise—that had soared above faraway parts of the world and looked down upon unimagined landscapes.

He saw it as he came up among the rocks marking the crest of the ridge. It was closer than he had guessed. A bend of the river curved toward the ridge leaving just a narrow, wooded slope, and the bird was sitting close to the water in a grassy area between the trees. He was staggered by the size of it, far larger than any bird he had ever seen—indeed, larger, surely, than any animal that he had heard of. Its feathers were the smoothest white, shining like a temple's marble walls in the sun, its wings surprisingly small, stretched back along its body and flaring at its tail like the vanes of a spear point. Samir kept low behind the rocks and stared in wonder. He decided that it was some unearthly breed of giant swan. It sat motionless, seemingly watching the river.

And then Samir's eyes widened, and he straightened up involuntarily. There was a human figure down there too—an armored warrior, from the look of him— moving barely several yards away from the Swan, but apparently taking not the slightest notice of it. There were other figures too, smaller ones: two at the river, another reaching up among some bushes by a stream.

Snatches of their voices carried up on the breeze. Children's voices. Samir couldn't make any sense of it. What were warriors doing in a place like this, and with children? Why should the Swan have come down to them?

Then, suddenly, another voice, a girl's, sounded from somewhere much closer. Before Samir could fix the exact spot or retreat behind cover, the bushes parted just a few yards away, and she appeared, talking over her shoulder to somebody following her. Her face was pale, like those of people who came from the north, her hair straight. She was wearing a peculiar reddish-brown, close-fitting garment with sleeves and legs, and holding a flower that she had picked. Behind her was an older girl, almost Samir's age, similarly clad in light green. She saw Samir first, and froze, staring, her mouth gaping in a silent cry, whether of surprise or terror, he couldn't tell. The younger girl saw her expression, turned, and instantly fell silent.

Samir couldn't take his eyes off the older one. Her skin had a smooth, almost ethereal fineness, devoid of any line or blemish, as if it had never felt heat from the sun or been roughened by wind or weather. Her hands were delicate and smooth, her face flawless, and her eyes had such a quality of innocence that Samir could have believed that she had stepped into the world just a moment ago. But what astonished him most was her hair, falling in soft waves to her shoulders, the color of finest gold. She could only be of royalty—a princess, even if unusually dressed for one; though what royalty could be doing here, he was unable to imagine. He forced a smile, as much as anything from an instinctive reaction that some justification was called for to excuse his own presence. "I . . . didn't expect to find anyone here," he said. The Princess didn't respond.

A heavier tread sounded, accompanied by the swishing of greenery being pushed aside. Moments later, the biggest warrior that Samir had ever set eyes on emerged behind her. The warrior stopped just as abruptly as had the child and the Princess. Samir got the odd feeling that the warrior was as confounded to see Samir as Samir was by the sight of him. He had to be seven feet tall, Samir judged, and was fully armored from head to toe, even his face. Over his upper body he wore a tight corselet, patterned in silver and blue speartips, hemmed at the waist by a belt carrying various accessories. The armor was more intricate and expertly fashioned than any that Samir had seen before, with amazingly complex arrangements of sliding joints around the shoulders and limbs, and individual eye visors that glittered like black gems. With relief, Samir noted that the warrior didn't appear to be carrying a weapon, although he had no doubt this was the Princess's bodyguard. A fourth figure had appeared in the rear, also—another child, about the same age as the first, this time a boy, wearing a blue suit, his skin almost as dark as charcoal. The children's faces as they regarded Samir were frank and curious, without hint of nervousness or fear—another sure sign of their royal origins. Samir began piecing things together. The Princess and these royal children, with handpicked champions to protect them, had come to this place to meet the Giant Swan from some godly realm. What had he intruded upon? He had no idea what it could mean.

The Princess and the warrior exchanged words in a tongue that Samir didn't understand. Their tone seemed to convey wonder and astonishment, not anger. That was something, anyway. The warrior moved forward and circled Samir slowly, studying him from all angles. Samir stood, waiting awkwardly, still trying to smile. He was acutely conscious now that in having spoken before being spoken to, he might already have breached propriety to a degree that was inexcusable. Were they merely curious as to this commoner's son, brazen enough to spy on dealings between royalty and the emissaries of gods? Or were they simply considering the most entertaining way to chastise him? Or worse.

Again the warrior and the Princess spoke incomprehensibly—in a way that sounded unlike any of the languages that Samir had heard but didn't speak. The Princess lifted her arms, and the warrior pointed at Samir's. Then he made a motion in the air that seemed to indicate Samir's form generally, gestured at himself, and then again made the same motion in the direction of the Princess. They seemed to see some deep significance in their all having the same shape. Now Samir thought he had the answer. They were travelers from so far away that they were not even sure they were still in lands inhabited by their own kind. Perhaps they were lost, and the Giant Swan had been sent to guide them. But the Swan had died by the river. Samir's spirits rose. In that case, maybe *he* could be their guide, he thought to himself.

Now he wished that Xeldro were here. Xeldro knew how to overcome the fears and suspicions of strangers, and was always well received wherever he went. "The first thing, give gifts," Samir remembered him saying. He felt about his person. He had a knife that he had crafted himself, but it seemed inappropriate for a princess and would surely be an insult to a warrior. In the purse hanging at his waist were a handful of mixed coins and some pieces of jewelry. The jewelry was cheap; he wouldn't risk offering that. He selected two small gold coins and squatted down on his haunches to offer them to the children. They exchanged more words with the Princess and the warrior. Finally the black-skinned boy approached, took the coin, and examined it curiously. Samir handed the other to the young girl. She hesitated, looked up and said something to the Princess; then, extending her arm uncertainly, she held out the flower that she had been carrying. Samir blinked perplexedly. What kind of trading was this— a gold coin for a crumpled flower? Then more of Xeldro's words came back to him: "No gift that wins friendship is ever a loss. It earns the greatest value that can be possessed." He took the flower and fastened it carefully to the collar of his tunic. The girl smiled.

And what for the Princess? Samir was at a loss. He dropped onto one knee, acknowledging her rank, and spread his hand to show that he had nothing that was worthy. The Princess said something to the warrior. She sounded uncertain, as if she were asking something. The warrior answered. And then the strangest thing happened that Samir had ever experienced in his life. The Princess dropped down onto one knee too, imitating him.

For several seconds Samir could do nothing but stare. What could this mean? Were they making a mockery of him? Had they come from a realm so distant that all the customs and ways of every land that Samir had heard tell meant nothing to them? And then he saw that she was smiling in a curiously anxious kind of way, watching his face searchingly . . .

She wanted to know if she was doing it correctly!

And *he* had been apprehensive. His relief, and a sudden sense of the absurdity of it all, came over him in such a flood that he couldn't help laughing. And the Princess laughed too.

They straightened up together. Yes, it was all right. Her smile was genuine. He pointed to his chest several times and said, "Samir." She looked at him questioningly. He repeated the gesture. "Samir."

"Sa-mir?" she repeated haltingly.

He nodded, then pointed at her. She looked at the

warrior, as if for confirmation, then back at Samir again. "Taya," she said.

"Taya," Samir said. He liked the name. He pointed to himself. "Me." Then at her again. "You. . . . Me, Samir. You, Taya."

She seemed to ponder this new information. Finally she pointed at herself. "Me?" Samir nodded vigorously. She caught on fast. Encouraged, she pointed at him. "You." He nodded again. "You . . . Samir."

Samir indicated the Warrior. "Him."

In the next few minutes, they started to get the hang of it. The warrior was called Kort. The two children were Cariette and Eltry. Samir was accepted. He had no doubt now that he could become their guide. But to do that, he first had to know where they were going, why, and a lot more about them. He would need to involve wiser heads than his, he realized. The first thing would be to bring them to the village of Therferry and confer with the elders. And Xeldro would be there too. In fact, if they left now and didn't waste time, they could catch Xeldro's caravan at the gorge where the road crossed over a narrow bridge, and ride the rest of the way in one of the wagons. Samir pointed back over the rise and made signs to Taya and Kort that they needed to go that way. They seemed to understand, and indicated that they concurred. Samir pointed past them down the slope, to the other figures by the Swan and the river, and beckoned for them to be brought up too. Kort turned his head and looked back, and a surprising thing happened. Nobody uttered a sound that would carry, yet the other warrior turned, just as if someone had called to him, and stared up in their direction. Seconds later, Samir saw him gesturing to the other figures and pointing up at the rise. They came together from different directions, four of them, Samir could now see—again, from their size, apparently all children—and with the second warrior leading, began ascending the slope.

Samir had no idea what strange manner of people he had chosen to become involved with, or what he might be getting himself into now. Maybe, if he served them well, they might even take him back with them to the realm whence they had come. But excitement at the prospect of unknown adventure surged through every nerve. No life of sweating cooped up in a smoky hut in the city could compare to this.

Behind them, at the bottom of the slope, the steps retracted into the lander, and its hull door closed. In the sky above, the probe moved from its station to follow their progress.

He was a boy, like Bron or Jasem or Eltry, yet bigger even than Taya. He wore a skirt of some coarse material with an open tunic and loose white shirt that showed muscles around his chest and shoulders that were larger and more solid than hers would surely ever be—although he showed no sign of the swelling at the breasts that Taya had experienced in the last few years, which none of the children showed yet.

His skin was darker than Jasem's but not black like Eltry's, and he had long, wavy hair and showed firm white teeth when he smiled. Also, he had a curious pointed tuft of hair growing on his chin, and more in a line below his nose. But, most important, his form was the same as that of Taya and the others, from which Kort had modeled his own. Could it be, then, that these were the Builders of the machines? It seemed to follow from the way the machines had always reasoned; and yet, nothing so far had hinted at the presence of what might properly be called a machine anywhere. But if the first machines had been built even before Merkon existed, surely they would be everywhere on Azure by now. There were a thousand things that Taya wanted to know, but Samir was in so much in haste to get wherever he was taking them that it seemed the questions—and how to express them—would have to wait.

Taya's legs ached already, and her breath was reduced to short gasps, as happened when she played games with the children and exerted herself too much. Nowhere in Merkon were there floors that sloped upward endlessly like this, with tangles of wire and water-plastic that caught her feet, hard lumps that rolled and shifted under her, or heaps of powder that she slid on or sank into. The wires had hairs and points that scratched her hands, sometimes drawing blood, sprang back across her face, and caught in her clothes. Her eyes were watering, and she was beginning to feel a soreness and rawness all over her face. The children were having the same problems, and had fallen silent except to grumble when one twisted a foot, or squeal at a pricked finger. Samir strode ahead effortlessly with laughs and encouraging gestures, seeming, if anything, to find their discomfort amusing. If this was some kind of game, Taya thought it was a mean one. She wasn't so sure, now, that she liked him as much as she'd thought. Kort, of course, was able to keep up with Samir easily, and was making better progress with the Azurean language.

"Kort, this isn't very nice for us," Taya said. "Do you know what he's doing?"

"The probe sees more Azure-life like Samir, and some four-legged forms, in a corridor ahead," Kort replied. "I think Samir is trying to meet them. It's not far now. Less than the distance we've come already."

"I don't think we'll ever get anywhere," Marcala said. "This just goes on for ever and ever and ever."

They passed a pool of brownish water with more wire and pointed ribbons standing in it. Bron stopped, pointing at something in the sticky paste stretching along its edge. "Come look at this. It's a walking chip." The others crowded around to stare. Something black and shiny with moving pins along its sides was scurrying over the globules. Taya couldn't decide if it was a circuit chip with legs or another life form. Samir called back and waved an arm to hurry them along.

And then, at the bottom of a slope of green carpet,

they passed below a wall of tightly packed yellow granules and came out suddenly into the corridor that Kort had described. It was nothing like a corridor in Merkon, of course—but it was long and open, and a lot flatter than the surfaces they had been crossing, though still lumpy compared to a real floor. It had irregular channels carved along it that looked as if they were for carrying water. Antennas and clumps of green bordered one side; the other sloped down steeply to a larger water channel. A short distance away, the corridor passed over the channel via a narrow strip that for once had the look of being "made." Still grinning, and looking as fresh as if he had just woken up, Samir made signs indicating that they had reached their destination and could rest now. The children flopped down on agglomerate lumps and pieces of carpet, gasping and sighing. Kort and Scientist stood, studying the surroundings. Taya sat on a cylinder lying by the side of the corridor, that looked like a fallen antenna trunk. Its surface was rough, with deep and intricate grooves. The material that it was made of was unfamiliar.

"I'm thirsty. Can we go and get a drink?" Cariette asked, looking down toward the water.

"We'd never climb back up *that*," Marcala said.

"I'll fetch some," Eltry offered. "Have we got anything to carry it in?"

Samir, watching, unhitched an odd-looking flexible bottle from his belt and offered it to Taya. She frowned at him and shrugged. He unplugged the top, raised it above his face and squeezed it to direct a spurt of water into his mouth, then offered it to her again. She copied him. The water was warm and had a strange, flattish taste, but was refreshing after the effort. Taya drank some more, then passed the bottle round among the others.

While Taya was doing this, Samir wandered over to some wiry constructions nearby and began picking at them. He came back holding a half dozen or so ovaloid objects, for the most part yellow, but reddish in places. Again he offered one to Taya. She took it and examined it curiously. It was cool and smooth like metal, but softer than metal. She looked up at Samir, smiled to show that she didn't doubt he meant well, and shrugged again. He seemed incredulous, and said something that carried a tone of telling her she couldn't be serious. She shook her head. Samir raised one of the other ovaloids to his mouth, bit a piece out of it, and chewed, making faces to show it was good. Several of the children gasped. Taya slowly imitated Samir's moves, nibbling just a tiny piece. The inside was wetter than she had expected, and sticky liquid trickled down her chin. The taste was sharp and sweet, with other flavors that she had no precedent for—stronger than any food she'd known in Merkon. She chewed warily, letting it touch every part of her tongue. There were sensations that were completely unfamiliar. As a first reaction, she couldn't make her mind up if she liked it or not.

Scientist took one of the ovaloids and broke it apart in his fingers, studying it intently. "Do you think you could make food like that?" Taya asked after watching him awhile.

"No, I'm not at all sure that I could," Scientist replied. He drew out the skin and internal membranes, seemingly perplexed. "But I might be able to *grow* it—in the same way that I grew you." He stared at the water-plastic structure that Samir had plucked the ovaloids from, turned his head to look again at the huge antennas, and went into a long, thoughtful silence.

4

The soldiers stayed well back, wary and apprehensive. Crelth urged his mount a few paces in front of them, equally reluctant to get too close. Everything about the beast was strange and unworldly. It seemed to emanate menace and evil. He felt himself being watched, as by a snake waiting for its moment to strike.

Fifty paces from pointed head to flared tail, he judged, bloodless white, the color of death, without feathers or down, the pale, cold skin of a cadaver. It sat as still as death even now, as aloof to the affairs of men as it was foreign to the world they belonged in. Slowly, he rode a wide path around it, his hand tight on the reins, ready to spring his steed away at the first sign of movement. Having inspected it, he would get himself hence, his orders carried out. What else could he be expected to do?

A shout from the river's edge turned his head just as he completed his circuit. Thankful for an excuse to put more space between himself and the Winged Death, he walked his steed over to where Udarth and several others had dismounted and were examining the bank. Udarth pointed to the mud. "Footprints. One set large, deeply impressed—a giant's. The rest smaller, maybe children's—two sets at least, could be more."

"Spread out. I want to know how much more this glade has to tell," Crelth ordered.

More small footprints were found in the sand by a stream running down on one side, from where a trail of trodden stems pointed to the overlooking slope. In a soft patch of ground partway up, another giant's print pointed away from the river. "Heading for the ridge," Udarth observed. "The only place within traveling distance that lies in that direction is Therferry."

Then that was where he would go, Crelth decided. At least it was a reason to get away from this accursed place and the presence that occupied it. He detached Udarth with five men to stand guard here, instructing him to send word immediately if anything developed. Narzin, who was the boldest and the fiercest, he made sure to keep with his own troop.

5

Kort spoke from where he was standing. "The other Azureans are here." Taya stood up from the trunk to face the direction that Kort was pointing. The children scrambled to their feet to look.

A line of bioforms was coming into sight around the bend in the corridor. As they approached, Taya saw that while some were similar to Samir, others were huge—bigger than mecbodies. The huge ones all had four legs. Some of them seemed to have two heads, while others, in pairs, pulled enormous boxes that rolled on wheels—similar in form to some of the toys the children had played with when they were younger. Samir moved to the center of the corridor, waving his arms excitedly and calling out a torrent of words. While Taya and the children stood speechless, the procession slowly drew nearer, finally drawing to a halt in front of them. One of the two-headed creatures divided itself into two parts, one of which descended and transformed itself into a two-legged form similar to Samir. The other head, much larger and completely different, remained attached to the part that had the original four legs. Taya was still trying to puzzle this out when another two-legged form climbed down from one of the wheeled boxes and began talking to Samir. He too had hair on his face, a lot more than Samir, crinkly and gray. He was heavier in build and wore more clothes, including a purple hat with a trailing piece that draped over his shoulders.

A long, animated exchange ensued between them, with frequent looks and gestures toward Taya, the children, and the two robots. While this was going on, Taya stared again at the four-legged form that had divided. Looking back at the two-legged part, then at the other forms still standing along the corridor, she began to doubt her first impression. They had never been one. The four-legged had been carrying the two-legged, in the way that Kort had carried her when she was young. She looked at it again, uneasily, taking in its huge head and mouth, swishing tail, and covering of coarse, matted hair. It smelt abominably. She couldn't help worrying about Biologist's speculation that bioforms might go through all phases serially. If this form carried two-legs, and Kort had carried her, did it mean that she and the children would one day turn into this?

Finally, Samir turned to Kort and launched into another exchange that involved gestures toward one of the boxes. "They want you and the children to ride," Kort interpreted. "Apparently there are others farther on that we are to meet, in a place they call 'village.' From what the probe sees, my guess is it's a group of Azurean living-cabins farther along the corridor."

"Farther?" Marcala wailed. "But we'll never, never, ever get back."

"That's all right," Kort said. "The machines can always bring the lander to us when we need to be picked up."

Encouraged by words and gestures from the Azurean two-legs, Taya and the children climbed up into the "cart." It contained bundles and chests, and also several more Azureans. Two of them were girls like Taya, but with cracked skin and white hair. One had hardly any teeth. They were much older than her, she guessed. Much, much older, yet still the same shape. Taya felt somewhat reassured. Maybe she wouldn't turn into a bad-smelling, four-legged hairy thing after all, she reflected gratefully.

6

Crelth was in a sour mood by the time he led his column into the village of Therferry. Now that his tension had eased, he was conscious of maybe having shown unseemly haste in front of the men in wanting to get away. He was angry at himself and spoiling for a fight to reaffirm his prowess.

Several colorfully painted carts and wagons were standing in the open space in the center of the village. Baggage animals were being unloaded, and others led into the communal corral to feed. Crelth recognized the caravan of Xeldro, the merchant, which had left Aranos the previous day. His orders were to be suspicious of merchants. They too easily made spies; their free and wandering way of life was not a good model for the people; and they lied to the tax collectors.

There was some kind of commotion in front of the house of the Headman, whom Crelth remembered from a previous expedition, though he was unable to recall his name, and a crowd gathered around. Figures ran ahead, warning of the approach of the soldiers, so that by the time Crelth drew up at the house, the Headman, several other village elders who had evidently been with him, along with Xeldro and his companions, were standing, waiting. There was another group too, who belonged neither with villagers or traders. Seven children in strange dress. Otherworldly dress. . . . Although one, in pale green, was taller than the others, practically a grown maid, Crelth saw on looking more closely. They all had strangely clear, otherworldly faces.

And standing with them were two enormous warriors covered every inch in armor. "Footprints . . . large . . . a giant's," Udarth had said by the river. Could there be any doubt that these were the silver ones of whom the King had spoken?

The Headman came to the front and bowed obsequiously. "Whatever pleases those who come in the King's name is our command, if it is within our ability to provide."

Crelth tested the children and the maid by fixing them with his sternest look. Not an eye among them dropped or averted. They continued to regard him with candor and curiosity, conceding nothing either to his rank or the armed might arrayed before them. Inwardly he was unnerved. It could only mean that their confidence in their two protectors was absolute. He felt his stature on trial in the eyes of the men behind him.

"Explain your association with these strangers who hide themselves in forests unannounced and call down beasts of death upon the land," he demanded, looking back at the Headman.

The Headman spread his hands helplessly. "Association? We have ourselves beheld them for the first time but a half the fall of an hour's glass since."

"Tis true," the elder next to him affirmed.

"Nearer a quarter of a glass," another said.

Xeldro, the trader, came forward and stood with them. With him was a youth, curly-haired, with a bright, intense look about him—sure sign of a troublemaker. Full of fanciful ideas about throwing off the duties conferred by birth, no doubt, and no knowledge of life. His chin could barely support the pretense of a beard.

"They arrived here with us," Xeldro said. "We came upon them on the road, tired, footsore, and without sustenance. 'Twas less than a league hence."

"Ah! And this meeting with spies and enemies, you would have us believe was mere coincidence?" Crelth challenged.

Xeldro showed his palms. "Where are these enemies of whom you speak? Canst not see these are but children?"

The youth stepped in front of him. "Travelers lost, sire. Royal heirs from distant, wondrous lands. 'Tis no beast of death that lies by the Ther, but a mighty swan that was sent to guide them."

So they knew more than they were telling, Crelth thought to himself. And their story was not consistent. If they had met these beings who posed as children on the road, how were they aware where the beast that had descended lay? The road was never in sight of that bend of the Ther river. Crelth signaled over his shoulder with a slight motion of his head to Narzin, who moved up alongside him. "Let us see how able these two champions are," he murmured. "Circle quietly about while I divert with words, then see if thou canst take one in sudden attack." Narzin returned a faint nod and fell back from Crelth's view. It was the only way to find out, Crelth reflected. And *he*, sure as Hades, wasn't going to risk it.

"A swan, sent to guide them where?" he asked the youth.

"That was the next thing I hoped to find out," the youth replied. "Perhaps, royal visitors to the King himself. Emissaries from rulers of other realms."

"What, on foot, lost, without carriages, baggage train, or servants? What manner of royalty travels thus?" Crelth directed his gaze at one of the two warriors, the one adorned in blue and silver. "Have you nothing to say on behalf of your charges?"

The warrior answered, "We outlanders. Simpler, if it pleases."

"They are unfamiliar with all the tongues of which I have knowledge," Xeldro said.

"From much more distant lands," the youth insisted.

"You have a name?" Crelth asked the warrior. Then again, "You? Name?"

"Name Kort."

"From where?"

"I regret."

"Place?"

"Explain 'place,' if it pleases."

The spear flew in from the side and struck the warrior below his right ear, emerging on the far side to lodge grotesquely through the neck like a spit skewering a piece of meat above a fire. Screams and

119

shouts of alarm broke out, and villagers scattered. Hoofs pounded as Narzin closed, swinging an axe and catching the warrior solidly in the side. The warrior fell, twisting so that one end of the spear struck the ground; he hung for a moment, then collapsed, his body bending double, almost cleaved in two. Narzin wheeled to face the other, while soldiers fanned out to encircle him with spears and bows. But the gray-coated warrior remained immobile, seemingly paralyzed. The child-impersonators too appeared to have lost the use of their faculties, and just stood, their faces frozen in shock. The village elders shrank back in consternation. Xeldro was shaking his head, looking dazed.

So . . . perhaps it had all been bluff after all. Crelth dismounted, unsheathing his sword. The youth broke through between the flanks of the horses and ran at him, his arms high in protest. "No! They are only children! You can't—" Crelth checked him with his fist and sent him reeling with a blow to the head from his sword hilt. Then he stepped over the prostrate warrior and hacked off his head. The maid in green came forward as if in a trance and gazed down between hands pressed in horror to the side of her face, seemingly incapable of making any sound. Crelth grabbed her arm roughly and shoved her toward other soldiers who had dismounted.

"Bring carts from the village and take all of them," he commanded. "The child-demons, the trader and his accomplices who consort with them, and the warrior who stands silent. All shall answer before the King personally in Aranos."

He looked down again at the slain warrior. The mail and corselets beneath the armor were the strangest he had ever seen. Curiously, there was no blood.

7

"Maybe they don't go through a simple progression of forms from smaller to larger," Biologist said. "It could be that as they evolve, the number of limbs gets less. See how the smallest forms have eight, six, and in some cases many more legs and other appendages. But the quadrupeds are all larger. I propose they go through a quadruped sequence from small to large that reaches the size of the forms that draw the wheeled constructions, and then recapitulate the process when they become bipeds."

"You mean they reduce in size again to go through the flying phase, and then grow once more to become biopeople?" Thinker queried.

"Yes. Something like that."

"So why didn't Taya and the others go through those phases too?" Skeptic asked.

"We grew them under different conditions," Biochemist said.

"Nobody's shown me how altering the conditions affects anything," Skeptic retorted.

"I still think they're different paths that radiate out in different directions from similar starting points," Thinker said.

"Why should the same speck of jelly turn into things that are so totally different?" Kort asked.

"Different director molecules," Biochemist offered.

"Taya and the others had different sets of director molecules too, but they all have the same body form," Scientist pointed out.

"Maybe there are other molecules that are different in ways we don't know about," Thinker thought.

"Show me some," Skeptic challenged.

"Perhaps Supermind just wills them to grow differently," Mystic mused.

Suddenly, Coordinator overrode all interactions with a general message flagged highest priority. "Emergency condition on surface. Azurean has deactivated Kort's body by means of total destruction. Action not deducible rationally from any accepted premises. Immediate analysis, please. Explanation and recommendations requested." The sequence recorded through Scientist's imagers was replayed.

Reactions poured in from the network:

"Deliberate destruction?"

"He meant it?"

"*The implements used seem devised for such a purpose.*"

"*Fear and excitability registering from other Azureans.*"

"*No computable long-term benefit.*"

"Leave the probe shadowing and bring the lander back up to Merkon," Coordinator instructed Engineer. "We need to get more bodies down there. Scientist, continue local observation."

"Will do," Scientist confirmed.

"Allocating a backup body to be finished as a replacement for Kort's," Scheduler advised.

"Restarting lander drives now," Engineer reported. "The six Azureans who remained in its vicinity are departing in haste."

8

Azure turned, and Vaxis sank lower. The strange, overhead sky changed from white and blue to gray and orange. Taya sat with the others in the cart, shivering despite the coarse blanket pulled around her shoulders. Azurean robot-people, part flesh and part metal, sitting on their four-legged carriers, rode on either side. Scientist was walking behind, attached by a strange ropelike garment he'd been given, secured around his neck. The Azureans had also tied his hands for some reason. He had complied without questioning or objecting. There was no point in getting another mecbody broken up. And Scientist was the only link that Taya and the others had to Merkon.

Several hours had gone by since their leaving Village. Taya hadn't recovered from her bemusement at what had happened. She was still grappling with the notion of damaging a person deliberately. No such concept had ever existed in Merkon. Oh, now and again the children might disagree over something and squabble or fight for a while; but those were invariably short-lived affairs not aimed at willful injury—apart, maybe, from a few slaps and pinches that never amounted to anything serious. Kort had been functionally destroyed. If it had been just some kind of gesture directed at a body that wasn't really Kort, Taya could have accepted it more easily. But the violence inflicted on Samir had been almost as malicious, gashing his head so that blood poured down over his clothes, and knocking him senseless. Never had Taya felt so exposed, threatened by unknown dangers from every direction. She thought of Merkon somewhere high above, and longed to be warm and secure again inside its enclosing walls. She would never come down to a planet again, she resolved. Planets were awful places.

And yet, there was something about the thought of going back to Merkon and not seeing Samir again that she found strangely disturbing. Even in those few hours, something about his smile, the way his eyes laughed—even the fact that he seemed practically the same age as her—had created a feeling in her that she had never experienced before, as if an emptiness would exist now if it were taken away. The Azureans had thrown him in the same cart as her and the children—the older hair-face and those who had been with him were distributed among the others. She looked down at Samir, his head resting on her knee. She had cleaned his wound as best she could with a cloth wetted from the water jug they had been given, and tied a covering over it. He had gripped her hand in a way she'd found oddly gratifying—not at all like her feelings when she held the children's hands to lead them, or to comfort them when they felt discouraged over something—and talked to her, though most of what he'd said she hadn't understood. Now he was sleeping again, and still she clung to his hand.

As the light grew less, they stopped by another corridor of flowing water—or maybe a different part of the same one they had left the lander by; Taya had lost all sense of direction. The four-legs pulling the carts were unhitched and tied along with the carriers to ropes that let them move over a wide area. To Taya's amazement, they began eating the green carpet that formed the floor. She remembered the yellow ovaloids that Scientist had said he believed *grew*. So were the green carpets that covered huge

125

areas of Azure also food that somehow grew? The idea of food *growing*—in the kind of way biolife did— was completely new.

The Azureans cut down pieces of antennas—which turned out to be not metal but formed of the same hard-packed grainy material that the carts were made from—collected them into piles, and to the children's astonishment set fire to them. They produced strange foods which they mixed and heated, then handed around in bowls. Some tastes were peculiar but interesting, others awful. Textures were varied: thick, porous wafers that softened when dipped in dark soupy mixtures; strips of crunchy fibers; pieces of stringy substance, with hard white parts that had to be thrown aside. Eltry enjoyed it the most. Marcala and Jasem were sick.

The sky turned black, and stars returned. The sight made Taya think again of the empty void, safe and familiar; of walls and floors that were built in straight lines; of light and warmth; of the machines. The Azureans directed her and the children back up into the carts to sleep. Before letting them settle down, they put metal anklets on them, with links to a chain attached to the cart. The intention seemed to be to prevent them from leaving. The anklets were uncomfortable and pointless. Where was there to leave for?

Marcala and Cariette pressed against her under the covers and fell asleep instantly, totally exhausted. On Taya's other side, Samir lifted his blanket over her and pulled her close, sharing their warmth. Despite the rigors of the day, the unnaturalness of everything around, and everything that had happened, she felt a strange contentment from his nearness.

When Taya awoke, the sky was gray, with water falling out of it. It was a new "day." After another meal, smaller this time, of more peculiar ingredients, the four-legs were attached to the carts again, and the journey resumed. They came to more open surroundings, covered increasingly densely by Azurean cabins made from cut-down antennas. Gradually, these gave way to larger constructions built from shaped mineral blocks, with flat slabs also covering the floor areas between. They were entering the "spread-out Merkon" closest to the landing site, that the probe had sent images of.

The procession passed through great doors in an immense wall, where more "soldiers" on four-legged carriers joined them. Inside, all around, the constructions were higher, more elaborate and more closely spaced, formed of huge slabs supported on columns, through-ways connected by arches, the main edifices rising to domes and pinnacles. Azureans by the hundred in colorful crowds thronged in the spaces between. This was a "city," Samir said. Its name was Aranos. It was where he was from. He asked the name of the place that Taya was from. She answered, "Merkon." Samir had never heard of it. Taya told him it was a city in the sky.

9

King Cyron felt relieved and more sure of himself now. The messenger had described nothing more menacing than a handful of disheveled children and two impotent knights, who had met up on the road with Xeldro and his rag-tag band of peddlers—whether by accident or design was not clear, but Cyron would find out. One of the knights had succumbed ignominiously, while the other was being led docilely in like a common peasant. Meanwhile, the flying creature that some claimed to have seen had deserted—if, indeed, it existed at all—and returned to realms that were no concern of men. In fact, Cyron found the news sufficiently reassuring to decide on a public display of his power and invulnerability as the most effective way of laying to rest speedily rumors that the seer, Serephelio, and his ilk, had been spreading.

Accordingly, Cyron gave instructions for the captives not to be taken directly to the jail, but paraded through the city to provide a spectacle for all. He, accompanied by his Chief Counsel, High Priest, and other officials of state would meet them in the Square of Avenues, before Royal Guards and troops from Gallestari's army, recently returned in triumph from Halsabia. Serephelio would be brought from the dungeons to confront his prophecies there, before the people, and let them see for themselves the absurdity of what they had let themselves be persuaded could ever have constituted a threat to Majesty or State. And besides, Cyron himself was curious.

He certainly didn't see much evidence of power terrible enough to shatter the nation and bring in the dawn of a new Age as his chariot and the carriages carrying the notables, flanked by their escorts, drew up in front of Gallestari's waiting ranks, where the prisoners had been arrayed. As the messenger had said, they were mere children—although Ishtelar had cautioned against the possibility of fiends taking the forms of children to deceive. But try as he might with his greatest efforts of imagination, Cyron was unable to ascribe the remotest hint of fiendishness to this motley collection. The crowd, now that their fears had been exposed as baseless, were keen to make light of it, as if to show that they hadn't really been misled. Their mood was buoyant, looking to be entertained. Very well, Cyron, thought. If they wanted a circus, he would give them one.

He climbed down from his chariot and advanced with a retinue of Guards and officers toward the captives. There were seven of them, including a girl somewhat older than the rest, yellow-haired and light-eyed—a witch if ever he'd seen one, prospective candidate for the stake on all their behalfs, Cyron noted mentally. They looked unkempt and dejected, with dirt-streaked faces, hair tousled, their clothes spattered with mud and still damp from the rain that had fallen that morning. The knight was formidable enough in appearance, sure enough, but stood unresisting, hands bound, guards holding him by two halters about his neck. Xeldro and his troupe stood alongside them, their heads bared and eyes downcast. A youth with a thin beard, his head bandaged, seemed unsure as to which of the two groups he belonged to. His glances betrayed an attachment to the yellow-haired witch. Two for the stake, Cyron thought.

Hands on hips, he strode slowly along the line, surveying them one at a time. "So . . ." he concluded, raising his voice to carry, "Is this the mighty host that I was told has come to vanquish Leorica?" Sniggers came from some of the crowd. The rest, sensing the atmosphere of the occasion, began to guffaw or jeer as the mood took them. Cyron let himself be drawn into the role. There were times when even a tyrant could afford to let up a little. He turned a full circle, his arms raised appealingly. "See, this warrior king has come to learn the ways of gentleness. Who are these who would keep Royalty waiting in vain? . . . I'm still waiting." He came back to face the captives. "When are the lessons to begin?" Laughter broke out all around. Some of the Guard officers grinned at each other. Cyron walked up to stare impudently at the knight, encased in his strange, total-body armor, the like of which Cyron had never seen before. But from what he had been told, it wasn't a lot of good. "I take it you must be one of the seer's gods," he said. Silence. "Are you a god? . . . Forgive me if I sound a little irreverent just at this moment. Perhaps I need more convincing. Won't you work just a little piece of magic or something miraculous to bolster my faith? I must confess that on occasion I find myself given to these moments of doubt. A failing of our lineage, I'm told. Still, I'm sure you can help me put matters right." The crowd were going delirious. Inwardly Cyron reveled in it, but he maintained a dignified exterior. "They don't seem to have much to say," he commented, turning to his officers. The cavalry captain who had sent the detachment to Therferry turned with an inquiring look to the officer who had led it—Cyron had ascertained that their names were Descemal and Crelth. Mounted behind Crelth was the huge, black-bearded figure of Narzin, his second, utterly loyal and without fear.

"They speak no known tongue, Majesty," Crelth answered. "The knight has mastered some of our words. But sparingly—permitting only the simplest of communication."

"Hmm." Cyron didn't want to lose effect now by letting things degenerate into labored repetitions of words and syllables. Serious interrogation would be more effectively accomplished later. He waved for Serephelio to be brought forward in his chains, at the same time nodding to Ishtelar in his carriage to speak. The High Priest rose, paused a moment for all attention to shift to him, and pointed an accusing finger. His voice echoed across the Square.

"This is the prophet who would spread falsehood among you!" The arm moved and quivered. "Here are the agents that you were told to fear and dread!" And moved again, to single out Xeldro. "There is he who was deceived into serving them, and his followers who let themselves be led on a path that leads to ruin." Xeldro was shaking his head in protest, but it would be of no avail. The situation demanded examples. Ishtelar continued, "Now you shall see what becomes of doubters and unbelievers, who surrender to weakness and allow false teachings and foolish fears to . . ." The High Priest's voice died away as he realized that a sudden agitation was robbing him of the crowd's attention. He frowned, sending a puzzled look at Cyron. Murmurings rose and swept across the Square. Arms pointed at the sky; faces turned upward. A noise like a sustained peel of distant thunder rolled down, mixed with an unearthly singing that could have been voices of the damned.

Cyron shielded his eyes with a hand. A shape like a squat, blunt-nosed dart was descending over the city. Against the cloud it appeared dark in color, but as it came closer revealed itself as shining white. Some kind of huge, soaring bird? It was larger than any bird that Cyron had ever seen. A dragon? The mutterings among the crowd were changing to cries of fear and alarm now. Impelled by some common instinct as in a herd sensing danger, a general movement began away from the central part of the Square.

" 'Tis the beast returned!" Descemal gasped, his eyes wide. "The same beast that flew over us yesterday!"

"The same! The same that I beheld, and which rose from the bank of the Ther," Crelth affirmed. Ishtelar, still on his feet in the carriage, stared numbly. The other dignitaries sat motionless, their mouths gaping. Growing larger moment by moment, the beast sank toward the center of the Square. Below it, the terrified crowd scattered, knocking over and trampling one another in their haste to get clear.

"Archers forward," Cyron snapped, jerking his head around toward the Guard commander.

"*Archers, forward!*" The command repeated above the rising din. Gallestari ordered his spearmen to advance and assume a ready stance, while a company of archers ran forward between their ranks, fitting arrows and taking aim. The captive knight raised his arms wide to show his bonds broken effortlessly. His two guards pulled at the halters and were dragged off their feet as the giant turned to face them. He snapped the ropes as if they were thread. Cyron's knees felt suddenly weak. He groped shakily for his sword. The dragon's wailing rose to a howl. It was lower now than the tops of the surrounding buildings.

"*Loose!*"

Arrows rose in a swarm and clattered uselessly off the beast's side. It came to ground in the space that had been cleared. A jaw opened, and more gigantic knights like the captive—two, three, four of them— emerged. Cries of delight and laughter went up among the demon children. Crelth pointed in horror at the knight leading. It had a tunic about its upper body of silver and blue, with black borders at the neck and cuffs. "The knight that was killed in Therferry! He is resurrected! Look, he returns from the dead!"

Serephelio's voice rose in the background. The prophet was standing with arms extended wide in their chains, face radiant, heedless of the gaolers trying to restrain him. *"Hear ye! It has come to pass! 'A new light will move in the sky, and gods of silver come down to walk among men.' . . ."*

Five spearmen closed around the captive knight, while others rushed forward to intercept the four from the dragon. Beside Crelth, Narzin spurred his mount and reached behind the saddle for his battleaxe.

Three projectiles were in the air and heading toward Scientist, of the same kind as the one that had pierced Kort's original body. He computed their impacts as 0.75, 0.92, and 1.3 seconds away. Also, the dark-chinned Azurean who had split Kort's casing with the edged implement was grasping it again and moving forward. But his estimated arrival was a comfortably long interval away, and his probable course too unpredictable as yet to warrant calculating with precision.

"Pointed at the leading end, weighted to carry over distance, and constructed to be stable in flight," Scientist sent back to the network. *"They are specially designed for this purpose. No other conjecture is consistent with all data."*

"What purpose?" Skeptic demanded. *"How could they have been designed to deactivate mecbodies when there are no mecbodies on Azure to deactivate?"*

"Just because we haven't seen any, it doesn't follow that none exist," Thinker answered.

"*Show me a mecbody that's native to Azure, and maybe I'll believe it,*" Skeptic said.

"*No, what I meant was, specially designed for Azureans to deactivate each other,*" Scientist explained.

"*Request retransmit,*" somebody sent. Scientist complied. A while passed while the other minds pondered.

Impact updates: 0.45, 0.62, 1.0 seconds, Scientist's local subsystem reported.

"*Possible reason?*" Coordinator invited.

"*Method of discipline/training based on negative reward principle, maybe,*" Thinker suggested.

"*But wouldn't such methods be excessively destructive to biobody tissues?*" Kort objected.

"*I agree,*" Biologist said. "*In fact, estimated damage levels could easily be sufficient to cause permanent cessation of all biological functions.*"

"*Which would negate your conjecture of negative-reward-based training,*" Skeptic told Thinker.

"*True,*" Thinker conceded.

"*Submit alternative hypothesis to justify deliberate infliction of possibly terminal damage coefficients,*" Coordinator invited.

"*None immediately apparent,*" Thinker responded.

Impact updates: 0.25, 0.42, 0.8 seconds. Scientist began raising an arm and opening a hand in anticipation of the first projectile. Several more were in the air and following the first three now, but still too far away to be concerned over unduly.

"*Is it conceivable that seeking advantage over others*

through the deliberate infliction of harm could be customary?" Moralist, who had split off from and worked closely with Mystic, asked.

"What kind of rational advantage could be gained?" Skeptic queried.

"Biominds are not always noted for their rationality," Mystic pointed out.

"Moralist may have a point," Kort said. *"All indications are that the damage inflicted upon the head of Samir by the Talking One was deliberate."*

"Its effect was to render immediate insensibility and a profuse loss of blood. Samir is still weakened from it," Medic advised.

"Recapitulate Samir's actions immediately preceding, for clue to possible motive," Thinker requested.

"Fear and excitement. Consistent with concern that harm would be inflicted on Taya," Scientist replied. He caught the first projectile in one hand and broke it with the other. The strain readings fed back from his arm sensors gave him a measure of the strength of the material that the object was made from. A quick scan of the videos from the other mecbodies showed that no biopeople were in the projected path of the second projectile. He commenced a coordinated movement that would twist his body out of its way, at the same time swinging an arm in an arc that would bring his hand edge-on to deflect the third.

"The otherwise inexplicable observation of Azureans covering parts of themselves with metal is consistent

with the hypothesis if the purpose is to afford protection," Thinker mused.

"Could be for ornamentation, resistance against abrasion, or for regulating thermal balance," Skeptic opined. *"Alternatives not eliminated. Hypothesis not proved."*

"The missiles that struck the lander were propelled by stored strain energy and travel more swiftly," Engineer announced. *"More of them, in various stages preparatory to release, are evident in the vicinity. Simulation analysis shows numerous possible hazards to Taya and the children, also the Azureans accompanying them. Suggest that a debate to plan joint preventative action be added to current agenda."* The recommendation was approved unanimously.

"First priority, interpose and intercept," Kort proposed. *"Second priority, embark biopeople in lander and evacuate. Follow with analysis later."*

The Dark-Chinned One, on his mount, was getting close and had commenced swinging the edged implement to build up momentum. Scientist computed the compound trajectory resulting from the motions of mount, rider, and object, sidestepped and turned inside the swing, seizing the implement and propelling it forward harder; at the same time, he used his other hand to lift Dark-Chinned-One at his rearpoint behind his center of gravity and impel him in the same direction. The Azurean's powers of anticipation were not great, and Scientist was able to detach him from his mount and send him sailing on his way with a surprisingly modest expenditure of effort.

For months Gallestari had been waiting and preparing for the right moment. His triumph had provided the pretext for bringing his army into the city, and by coordinating his actions with the invasion that would follow the alliance he had formed in Halsabia, he had expected to overthrow Cyron within a week. But now, perhaps, an opportunity to make a better alliance was staring him in the face.

These gods—for surely they were, Gallestari was almost ready to believe—were returning Cyron's mockery multiplied a hundredfold, making his elite Guard look like clowns. Even as Gallestari watched, the knight, whose disdain was such that he could afford to amuse children by letting himself be led like a buffoon, threw off bonds that would have held a bull, danced unscathed amid hurtling spears or dashed them aside, and sent the cavalry captain's champion crashing to the ground as he would have tossed aside an irritating puppy. The knight of blue and silver that the Guard officer had declared resurrected called to the children, who began running toward the dragon. The three others who had been borne to earth with him passed between them to face the soldiers. Cyron's archers discharged a ragged volley. The arrows that threatened no one passed freely, while those that would have found marks were snatched from the air. Still these gods were playing games. And unarmed!

"Guards to the attack! Stop them!" Cyron shouted desperately. The royal elite came forward, brandishing spears and unsheathing swords. Gallestari swiftly assessed the situation. Hadn't his objective all along been to come out on the winning side? The moment, it was plain to see, was now. He made his decision.

"Third Infantry," he ordered. *"Block the Guards. Defend those children!"*

Amid battle cries and crashings of swords on shields and armor, the regular troops closed with the palace guards. Spears and arrows flew every way in the confusion. In the midst of all, the knights swayed and gyrated, snapping blades and plucking any missile out of flight that threatened their charges. Then one of the running girl-children fell. The yellow-haired maid, who had been urging them on toward the dragon, turned back and stooped to haul her up again, but Cyron in pursuit was upon them, his sword already swinging. Gallestari launched himself at them, but knew even as he moved that he would be too late. The nearest knight had started to twist back, but his balance was in the wrong direction; the split-second he would need to consolidate was too long. Behind Gallestari, Descemal saw the general moving on Cyron and aimed his spear. Another figure, the bearded youth, came out of the melee, and throwing himself in front of the maid, took Cyron's blow. Cyron heaved him aside as he fell, and freed his sword, but Gallestari reached him and plunged his own blade into his body before he could thrust again.

Cyron's eyes widened as he sank to his knees, recognizing his assailant. "*You* . . . would betray me? . . ."

"I serve mightier masters now," Gallestari hissed. And Descemal's spear hit him in the back.

Gallestari was on the ground, looking up while the maid stared in horror and shouted something to the knights. One of them picked up the youth and carried him into the dragon. Another stooped over Cyron, seemed to deliberate for a moment, then picked him up too and followed. Gallestari's head dropped against the paving. The last thing he remembered was a massive silver foot planting itself close by; pain searing even more intensely through his back as the shaft of the spear was broken off; metal hands gripping his shoulders and lifting him. . . .

10

Cyron had died and entered the Afterworld. It was nothing like the Afterworld that priests, shamans, and other self-styled authorities had described. He had long entertained suspicions of all of them. Their Afterworlds had been all-too-obvious imitations of the familiar Presentworld to be believable. The real Afterworld was unlike anywhere he had been, totally removed from any description he had ever heard, beyond anything that unaided imagination could have created.

There was no land or sky here, no mountains or ocean, trees or rivers, nor earthly creatures of any kind. Indeed, how could there be? Those were the things that made up the world of life, while this was the world that came after life. It floated among the stars, a maze of passageways with walls of jewels and metallic lusters, and chambers of light containing structures of complexity and purpose that defied comprehension. Here, magic reigned on every side. Darkness transformed into light without bidding; doors opened of their own accord; silver wands made water that was hot without fire; unharnessed chariots sped silently in tunnels through the labyrinth. Images that moved and spoke in crystal windows revealed mysteries the like of which in his entire mortal span he had never known.

He was visited often by the silver gods that had descended, whose domain this was—and the children, now restored to godliness, equally clearly in their natural realm. There were more of them than the few who had come down to earth on the dragon. Gods and children alike schooled themselves in Cyron's language and plied him with questions about himself, his world, and its ways. His first reaction was that they were joking at his expense, taunting him—for wouldn't gods already know all such answers? They fed him—strange foods, but what else was to be expected?—tended him, and brought spirits made of glass and shining metals to perform rites over his wound. He assumed this was preparation for later torture and torments as would be a prisoner's normal lot; but their power was so complete as to require no proof or demonstration, and they had no fear of him to be assuaged.

Instead, as their knowledge of his language grew daily, they listened in rapture like the children and grandchildren he had never known to stories that he told them of monsters and giants, cities and princes, magic lands and unmapped islands. They taught him of the strange realm of titanic forces and unimaginable distances that extended among the stars, in which the whole of earth was as a dust speck in a maelstrom. They introduced him to their games. Cyron saw how they received him in their world, and he remembered how they had been treated when they came to his. And for the first time, he felt shame. At night he lay awake, wishing that he could live again and put right as much as he could of the wrongs he had committed.

And then, one day when the spirit had bound his wound and he was feeling stronger, a new secret was revealed to him. The gods, in their benevolence, had not denied him companionship of his own kind. The general, Gallestari, had also died on that day in the Square of the Avenues, and had been brought to this same place. But such was the wisdom of the custodians that the two of them had been kept apart until their understanding was complete, and their enmity abated.

They sat in a glass-sided chamber, looking down from the black heavens over the shining blue world they had known. Every familiar coastline and ocean was there, and beyond them more, vaster, unheard-of regions than either of them had ever suspected. It was as if the pettiness and insignificance of their entire former lives lay spread out before them for their contemplation.

"The palace that was the greatest of my aspirations, the building of which consumed a thousand precious lives," Cyron said. "And my eye is unable even to discern it. Is that the measure of what I lived for? Yet mountains that are the palaces of eagles extend from sea to sea. So which has the monument that will endure eternally, and which is as good as already forgotten?"

"The empire for which I would have sacrificed whole nations lies hidden by a cloud," Gallestari answered. "The empire that the forests command knows no bound. So which is everywhere victorious and invincible, and which shall be swept away tomorrow as hoofprints in sand by the rain?"

The cryptic message was plain to Cyron now—why the gods had chosen to appear in the forms of destitute children. "The only history that has meaning is the growth of goodness in the hearts of men," he reflected. "The mother baking bread to feed her young ones

143

does more to write it than all the works of kings."

"Untold death and suffering, serving no end but to satisfy greed and vanity," Gallestari said. "Any farmer or fisherman, or artisan who builds a house or makes a shoe creates more true worth by every hour. The gods defeated us without inflicting injury or use of arms, showing that violence has no value. They took no side in our quarrel, show kindness in place of malice. Are we not taught that hatred is fruitless also?"

Cyron stared down over his former dominion and found the line of the Ther River, picking out the spot where Aranos would be. He thought of the aging prophet that he had dismissed as insane. Would he be free now, preaching his Word to the city's crowds? "And the Warrior Kings will learn ways of gentleness," he repeated to himself distantly.

And that was when the god who was called Kort appeared and informed them that the god Medic had pronounced them sufficiently recovered to go home. Neither Cyron nor Gallestari were sure what this implied. To their amazement, it turned out that his prayer had been heard. They were being returned to the mortal realm. Cyron could only assume that "recovered" meant reformed in their ways, their eyes opened now, fit to set example and carry the wisdom of the gods back to the world of men.

For them, the task was appropriate. They both had amends to make. The youth, Samir, however, would not be going back with them. Medic said there was nothing to be done. Cyron took this to mean that Samir's work was complete, and he would go on to the Afterlife that he had earned.

11

And so, as had happened with the god Kort, Cyron and Gallestari were resurrected from the dead. The city had been in tumult, with rival factions contesting and the army's loyalties divided to determine who would succeed. But the dissension melted away when the white angel carrying the invincible silver gods descended again, and the king and general who had died were delivered back to their people.

Forborem, Chief Counsel to the Throne, asked what was to become of the five thousand prisoners still being held, that Gallestari had brought back from his victory. "Feed them, dress their wounds, give them clothing and provisions, and send them home to their families," Cyron replied.

Taya stood by the city gate with Kort, Scientist, and Geologist—a new entity—watching the column of released prisoners leave. Xeldro was with them, and Serephelio. Taya was still grappling with the realization that Samir wouldn't be coming back. The thought produced an emptiness inside which she didn't understand, that wouldn't go away. And then again, for the last few days she had been feeling strangely weak and lethargic, with aches all through her body and flashes of sweating heat alternating with shivering cold. Perhaps that was what was giving her such odd feelings about Samir. She wasn't sure.

Azureans seemed able to accept such things more matter-of-factly. Apparently they believed that the same thing happened inevitably sooner or later to all life. But it had only happened to four of the biopeople in Merkon. Maybe Azureans thought that because they didn't have the technology to fix biobodies when they were damaged, Taya told herself.

But that was something they could worry about another day, she thought, as she watched the line of figures with their staffs and bundles and the pack animals they had been given, moving slowly away along the road leading from the city. The inhabitants of most of the houses had come out to watch and see them on their way. Their faces showed goodwill and sympathy. Some sent encouragement with a nod, a wave, or a friendly word. It all felt, Taya thought, more like the way things should be.

And there was elation on the face of Serephelio too, she saw, as he looked at the scene and took in its meaning.

The last part of the prophecy of old was fulfilled.

Peace had come upon the land.

THREE DOMES AND A TOWER

The wind rose and fell in squalls, carrying sea spray and spatters of raindrops from the overcast sky. Taya gripped the rail with one hand and pulled the hood of her padded overjacket closer around her face. A mile behind the boat, crumbling ice cliffs brooded over waves tossing restlessly beneath banks of mist. The snowfield above the ice cliffs rose in smooth slopes and ridges toward the jagged outcrops of the distant coastal range. Ahead, beyond the mouth of the bay, several smaller islands of the polar archipelago lay amid gray water flecked with floating ice debris and occasional larger bergs. The offshore platform, known simply as the "Rig," stood closer in, on a bank that formed an underwater continuation of the headland.

The boat was called a *caloosh*—a converted war galley, stripped of its masts, sails, and benches for rowers, with a strengthened hull and plasma-electric propulsion system devised by Engineer. Taya stood on the raised prow, forgoing shelter to study the Rig better as they approached. With her were Spak,

Engineer's local supervisor of operations, wrapped Azurean-style in a long coat of sealskin with fur trim, and Vaysi, wearing an orange one-piece thermsuit. Nyelise had stayed in the warmth of the aft cabin with its plastic-sheeted windows, in the company of the two Azureans and Kort. Although Kort's current body was ornamented in the same style of silver and blue points as the original, like the other Mecminds, he had taken to wearing clothes in Azure's more variable and extreme conditions. They protected against dust and abrasion, and were easy to clean and replace. Currently he was in a tan boiler suit with plastic boots to keep the salt water out of his joints.

Taya and Kort, along with Nyelise and Vaysi, had flown overnight from Aranos to "Icebowl," the arctic scientific base set up a year previously in a shallow basin on the reverse side of a ridge about a mile inland from the cliffline, above the pattern of ice movement. By local time it was mid-morning, although at that time of year darkness lasted little more than two hours. They had lunched with Spak and several others of the staff, who had updated them on the current state of the work. Afterward, two power sleds had brought them to the pontoon shore station beyond the cliffs, where a boat was waiting to take them out to the Rig.

The Rig had the approximate shape of a truncated pyramid. Three steel piers, braced by girders and cross-ties, converged upward from the water to support the main platform thirty feet or so above the surface, upon which was built the superstructure. A central column beneath the superstructure contained the twin elevator shafts, ventilation pipes, and supply lines to the lower workings on the seabed. On the far side from the approaching boat, four barges tethered side by side lay below hoppers that obviously discharged the rock and debris brought up from the excavations.

The pier nearest carried a floating dock with stairs and a hoist up to the main platform. A projection of the platform on one side formed a landing pad for short-range flyers, of which Icebowl boasted a permanent complement of two. One, however, was undergoing maintenance and the other was away ferrying supplies to one of the outposts on the ice sheet, which was why the visitors were coming out by boat.

"It's bigger than I expected," Taya commented. "Those legs look thick enough to shore up a mountain."

"They're on pilings that go through to bedrock," Spak said.

"I thought it would just be something like a drilling tower sticking up out of the water."

"The seas can get pretty heavy, especially in winter."

"Do you still get problems with bergs being carried this way?" Vaysi asked him. This was her third visit to Icebowl.

"Not so much. That idea we had for deflecting them with water jets worked out pretty well."

Taya had been amazed by the amount of materials and components had gone into the construction of Icebowl Base and its offshore extension. Everything had to come from the extraction and fabrication plants that machine intelligences linked to Merkon had set up at various places around Azure. There were only a few dozen of them, and their output was never enough to satisfy the demands of all the activities that were going on. The last twenty years had been a time of intensive invention and discovery. The machines had had no knowledge, nor even any concept, of mining raw materials and refining metals out of ores; indeed, before setting foot on Azure— or at least, sending down the initial probe from orbit— they hadn't even known what a rock was. In many ways they had learned as much from the natives as the Azureans had from them. Progressing from those beginnings to the development of methods to shape steel into forms like those used in the construction of the Rig, or make parts such as those that the motors driving the boat were assembled from, had taken most of that time.

"What would the people down there do if you did lose everything topside?" Taya asked.

"Well, we always bring everyone up as a matter of routine when there's a bad forecast. Then they have an underwater lock that they could use as an escape chamber." Spak shrugged and glanced at her with the confident grin that made him a natural as an organizer and leader. "I guess they'd just have to put on breathers and swim up, and trust us to get to them before the cold did."

Spak was one of the original forty-six Merkon "Primaries," or "Star Children," as most Azureans still called them. Now aged thirty-one along with the rest of his generation, he had developed an early desire to know more of the story of the Azureans, who had somehow originated on a planet, and devoted himself to piecing together their history. The Azureans themselves had never applied systematic methods of inquiry either to this field or to any other—nor indeed formed any such concepts, although many of them had proved to be rapid learners.

What had begun as simply an interest in the Azureans and their past became Spak's dedication as the arrivals from space learned of the widespread evidence that existed of a long gone civilization, referred to by the Azureans simply as the "Ancients," that had once existed on the planet. Although widely distributed, the traces were all but obliterated: the remains of a structure of some kind, uncovered by erosion in a river canyon; a rusted implement turned up by a plow; fragments of what were undoubtedly mechanical and electrical parts brought up from a quarry. None of it meant nothing to the Azureans. Evidently, a culture with knowledge of technologies far beyond the understanding of the present inhabitants had once flourished across the planet. Thinker had been the first to voice the obvious question of whether the Ancients and the "Builders"—the unknown creators of Merkon—had been one and the same. Spak had spent much of the years since then trying to find the answer. His specialized interests made him an obvious choice for coordinating the operations at Icebowl, and he had been there since its inception.

Not all of the original forty-six who arrived with Merkon had survived. There was no way that Scientist could have known about pathogenic microbes and the hazards of a competing biosystem. Sickness had swept through the children with every group that ventured out into the planetary environment, which by the time it became apparent that something was very wrong meant practically all of them. Eleven died in the first six weeks. Little Cariette, Taya's walking echo from that first group to land on the surface, had been one of the earliest. Bron another. The four isolated failures that had occurred long ago when Merkon was still years from the end of its voyage had not been sufficient for anyone to draw the general inference. Only on Azure did the newcomers learn that mortality was the inescapable price of biological life. That realization had been almost as much of a shock to them as the losses.

Three more—a number that could easily have been far worse, considering their naivete in a world filled with predators and all manner of hazards that nothing had prepared them for—had been lost in accidents since.

But then, as if it were Nature's way of compensating, they had reached the age of discovering life's miraculous process for renewing itself and producing fresh, impressionable minds, untrammeled by a lifetime's accumulated habits and prejudices, free to absorb new ideas. For the most part, "Merkonians" had adopted the practically universal Azurean custom of pairing, and being young and zesty they tended to be prolific. Vaysi, just turned eighteen now, was among the first of the second generation to be born, both her parents Primaries. She was a child both of space and of the planet, as much at home riding through forests with a hunting party of Azureans as conversing with machines up in Merkon. Her family of seven siblings lived among the Azureans in what had been a rival kingdom to the south of Leorica, practicing and seeking ways to improve the Azurean arts of cultivation. Vaysi had studied soils and how they were formed, which led to a curiosity about rocks and hence trying to understand the processes that had shaped the planetary surface generally. The Azureans had tended to apply themselves little to physical geography, focusing their attention on mapmaking and other arts more relevant to the advancement of war and conquest—of which the inhabitants of Merkon had no concept. But with Cyron's conversion and the continuing spread, after his death, of Leorica's new creed of peace and tolerance into the adjoining lands and beyond, such practices and the misery they created were disappearing. Instead, the world was discovering cooperation, trust, and the value of learning. In twenty years, partly through the analytical powers of the machines but due also to curiosity inspired among the Azureans themselves, more had been pieced together concerning the planet's past than had been contained in all the myths, legends, superstitions, and half-truths in circulation at the time of Merkon's arrival.

Whatever fate had overtaken the Ancients had been sudden and cataclysmic, involving upheavals of unimaginable violence and planetwide in extent. Remains of buildings and other constructions were found piled in gorges and rock fissures, or crushed beyond recognition under rock and compacted mud sometimes hundreds of feet deep. However, there were scattered coastal areas where for generations fishermen had been dredging up samples of advanced artifacts in a relatively undamaged condition from the seabed. Sailors told tales of similar objects being found frozen into the ice of drifting bergs, but most Azureans discounted them. Historian—extending his role to take in Azure's past as well as that of Merkon—had been curious all the same, and persuaded Scientist to mount several expeditions to investigate, in which Spak and some of the others had participated. Some icebergs had indeed turned out to contain machined artifacts, along with pieces of alloys, plastics, and other advanced materials. The currents that bore those bergs were plotted and traced back to their northerly origins. . . . And Icebowl Base had been established as a result.

Taya had kept to a solitary path over those years, refraining from emotional attachment or commitment to any one person. As had been the case since their earliest days in Merkon, Kort was her constant companion. Her uniqueness in Merkon had created a surrogate mother relationship directed equally toward all her charges, which would not be displaced. On top of that, the traumatic discovery of violence and death, and their deliberate infliction, all in rapid succession and which none of her experience had prepared her for, then culminating in the brutal ending before it had barely begun of the first hint of intimate affection that she had ever known, had been too much for her psyche not to react against self-protectively. The children had been resilient enough to absorb the shock and adapt to the new terms that life demanded. Just the few years separating them from her had been enough to make the difference.

In keeping with the role of guide and counselor that she had always filled, she had stood apart and watched while a new generation appeared and grew, some of pure Primary parentage, others from Azurean intermingling. The Azureans referred to the mixed offspring as "sky-blooded." It both astonished and delighted them that the Star Children who found unions beyond their own kind did not restrict themselves to the Azurean nobility and high-born, but followed their own instincts in judging what qualities constituted human worth. The Azureans were eagerly learning and adopting these new scales of values. To have one of the sky-blooded added to its numbers came to be one of a family's greatest sources of pride, and esteem among others. Most Azureans didn't comprehend Taya's relationship to her younger kin. To them she was simply the "Star Mother."

The two Azureans emerged from the cabin at the aft end of the boat, one of them coming forward to uncoil a line in preparation for docking. Taya watched him, his face leathery from the sun and weather, trying to picture how he and the generations before him had lived over the years, without machines or power, here in this land of frozen mountains and windswept snow. How much had those dark, narrow eyes seen that she would never know? Did the mind that looked out from behind them even perceive reality in the same terms as she? Scientist had been intriguing her with accounts of how the "true" reality of the physical world was nothing more than dancing patterns of energy quanta: all the impressions which together made up the reality experienced by consciousness—of biolife and machines alike—were somehow created by its own internal processes. Taya had been amazed that any two minds managed to see anything similar at all.

Spak pointed suddenly past the mouth of the bay, in the direction of the open sea. "Look. Whales!" Taya and Vaysi followed his extended finger. Two black, rounded shapes were coasting among the whitecaps beyond the headland. "They probably picked up the sound of the boat and came to investigate," Spak said. "Chel says they make strange sounds of their own. He thinks they might communicate that way."

Chel was another of the surviving Primaries, working most of his time with Biologist at trying to explain the diversity of Azurean life forms. Evolutionist had long ago conjectured that chemical life originating on a planet might progress from the simple to the complex. But whatever scheme was devised for arranging and categorizing them, the forms that existed on Azure showed no persuasive evidence of any progression. Even at the level of their molecular chemistry, all were equally complex. Thinker was baffled, and Mystic had gone back to claims of creation by Supermind. For the time being, none of the minds had a constructive suggestion to offer.

"Did you ever see whales before, Taya?" Spak asked.

Taya shook her head. "Not for real. Only pictures." As she watched, one of the whales vanished for a few seconds, then surfaced again, spouting water. "Chel told me that they're not really fish," she said.

Spak nodded. "I heard that too."

"What makes Chel say that?" Vaysi asked curiously.

"Apparently there's an Azurean he knows who's spent his life trying to find a system for classifying animals," Spak replied. "That was what he said, and when Chel checked it out, he was right."

"So what are they?" Vaysi asked. Spak shrugged and shook his head.

"I know that air-breathing was part of it," Taya said. She drew a pad from her coat pocket and spoke into it. "Kort, why does Chel say that whales aren't fish? Tell me the reasons again."

"Because they're air-breathing and maintain warm blood," Kort answered from the rear of the boat. "They bear their young live and nurse them the same way that practically all land animals do. Biologist says that relates them more closely to animals than to fish."

"Okay. Thanks." Taya glanced inquiringly at Vaysi.

Vaysi still didn't look happy with it. "Why should something that looks like a fish and swims like a fish be more closely related to pigs and tigers?" she challenged. Taya shook her head in a way that said she couldn't add anything to what Kort had told them.

"Does it make sense to you?" Vaysi asked Spak.

"How do molecules assemble into brains and feathers? If the Ancients could build Merkon, what happened to them? There isn't much about Azure that does make a lot of sense right now," Spak answered with a sigh.

Two more Azureans, wearing hooded furs, were waiting on the floating jetty at the bottom of the steps leading up to the platform. The *caloosh* came around, slowed to a bobbing crawl through the waves, and docked with a mild bump. The Azurean at the bow threw the line. One of the two who were waiting caught it and made fast to a mooring stanchion, while the other tied a second tossed by the Azurean at the stern. Kort and Nyelise came out from the cabin onto the deck. Taya, Vaysi, and Spak descended from the prow and went back to the midships section, where the hull ran against the jetty. The steel mesh of the landing stage was crusted with ice, and the Azureans who had tied the lines helped the arrivals as they clambered down the boat's side. "Careful, Kort," Taya cautioned. "You know that swimming is one thing that you people aren't exactly best at."

"Hmmph."

Seven mecbodies had been lost so far in accidents of one kind or another involving deep water. With things to attend to everywhere, most of the Mecminds possessed multiple bodies which they controlled simultaneously, generally scattered all over Azure and up in Merkon. To begin with, the different versions had been distinguished by numbers, but that had quickly become too impersonal and drab. So now they used their generic names along with individual identifiers chosen to be displayable as emblems that they carried on their shoulders for easy recognition. One of the Engineers—"Engineer Wrench"—had gone down in this very bay in Spring, when an Azurean barge came apart after being squeezed between two ice floes. Mecbodies had not been designed to be watertight.

Three sets of steel stairs brought them up to the main platform. Picking their way through an impossibly cluttered scene of pipes and machinery, overhead gantries, and stacks of materials waiting to be sent down, they came to the entrance into the superstructure. Another Merkonian, two more Azureans, and a Mec were waiting there. The Merkonian, clad in a parka almost as dark as his face so that only the whiteness of his grin made any contrast, came forward and greeted Taya and Nyelise with hugs that were warm in sentiment even if somewhat clumsy in their heavy clothes.

"Eltry, hello! It's been so long." Taya stepped back and looked him up and down, smiling. It must have been over six months since she had seen him. "Do you know, I swear you haven't stopped growing yet."

"On seal meat and fish? You've got to be kidding. It's all in the coat and the hood. Don't fool yourself."

Eltry's subject was Azurean languages—there were scores of them—art, and religions. He had been at the station since early Spring. Taya wasn't sure what interests of such a cultural nature he had found to detain him here. Mystic attached deep significance to the fact that just about every Azurean culture seemed to possess some version of belief paralleling his own, in a transmaterial realm of existence.

"Taya thinks we're all still children," Vaysi said, stepping forward. She and Eltry clasped hands through their gloves.

"Good to see you back, kid," Eltry said. He introduced the Azureans with him as Gorso, one of the tunneling crew foremen, and Karthel, a young woman of the northern "Usquil" race, from the local tribe that had helped build Icebowl. She apparently had an aptitude for electronics. The Mec was Engineer Moon, wearing blue coveralls and a peaked cap with a neck flap behind.

"I take it the flyer isn't back yet," Eltry said to Spak as he turned to lead the way inside.

162

"It was late getting away," Spak answered, following behind. "Krinji waited till the last moment to send through a revised list of things he wanted, and they had to change the whole load."

"Typical. I'm sure half these people still think we do magic. How's the other flyer at base shaping up?"

"Just a cracked heat shield to replace. It should be done by tomorrow."

As Kort had discovered long ago in Merkon, human hands were amazingly dexterous. For reasons the machines had never really understood, Azureans were fascinated by engineering and took a delight in learning how to make simple repairs and change parts.

The party entered an antechamber where furs and oilskins hung on racks, and boots, caps, ropes, and tools filled the remaining space. Spak found some room for the arrivals to leave their outer clothes. "It gets hotter farther on down," he explained. Taya hung her coat next to his sealskins and Vaysi's thermsuit, and smoothed out the gray cloak she was wearing underneath. A cloak of some form or another had remained her habitual dress through all the years that had passed since the Primaries were resuscitated.

Eltry opened an inner door, letting through a sound of voices from the far side. The noise continued for a moment, then died abruptly as somebody said, "I think she's here." Sounds came of chairs being pushed back and bodies rising awkwardly to their feet. Taya and her companions followed Spak into a cramped messroom, where a dozen or so figures in Merkon-style clothes—popular generally by this time—and Azurean smocks or belted tunics were standing among chairs and benches lining the walls, and on either side of a long table in the center. After the cutting freshness of the sea air outside, Taya almost choked at the sudden heat and fug of hot machine oil, cooking smells, and confined humanity, but managed not to show it. An urn was steaming in one corner. A screen at the far end showed chariot racing coming in live from Aranos.

Taya was used to stares, awed looks, and writhing faces desperately trying to look at ease and force smiles. It was the first time that most of them had seen the Star Mother. Spak announced her to the company, introduced Nyelise and Kort, and reminded them who Vaysi was, although most of them had already recognized her. Taya and her companions stayed long enough to be polite, chatting and asking questions. Some of the company seemed astonished that close-up she looked as normal as anyone else. They all took turns shaking her hand. A roar of delight went up on her behalf when the winner of the final was announced as Aranos's reigning champion. Finally, the party moved on.

A short passage between equipment compartments brought them to the central shaft housing the elevators. It was eighty feet down to the caisson on the seabed, where the main generators, elevator machinery, and air recirculation plant were housed.

The tunnel itself began thirty feet farther below that.

Test borings through the ice had yielded numerous artifacts and fragments similar to those recovered from drifting bergs and the seabed farther south, but only crushed and unrecognizable remains of the buildings and larger structures that had been hoped for. However, echo soundings and magnetometer studies indicated an area of extended objects deeper in underlying rock. The constantly shifting ice covering made impracticable any thought of exploration by direct mining operations from above. Engineer's solution: Sink an offshore shaft to below the ice level and tunnel back inland through the permanent strata beneath.

Or perhaps "more permanent" would have been a better way to describe them. One of the big questions, of course, was how this city—for by this time, that was what it was accepted as having been—of the Ancients came to be buried under all that rock. It was named "Vrent," after the mythical abode of a deity celebrated by the Usquils inhabiting that region. Geologist had determined that the rock was a soft, young variety compared to the kind that most mountains, for example, were composed of—almost a compacted clay not yet fully dried out. His theory was that it had been deposited by immense flooding in the not-far-distant past. Interestingly, different cultures all over Azure had legends of enormous floods prior to a later era of universal fire and exploding mountains known in Leorican lore as the "Conflagration."

They emerged from the elevator into a domed chamber shored with steel props and cross bracings, where bright lights above and on the walls illuminated bewildering tangles of pipes and cables, with machinery squeezed wherever the limited space would permit. Stacks of materials waiting to be sent forward were piled between cars full of digging debris to be taken up; and in every corner and cranny that was left, partitioned areas providing working and bench space. Spak led the way to the far side of the chamber, where doubled I-beams supported on pillars framed the tunnel mouth. A "mecroid" tractor—a general term for machines possessing enough code to function autonomously, but lacking the awareness of a Mecmind—was waiting in front of the opening, towing two open cars in tandem. The cars were the same pattern as the ones used for hauling rock, but with improvised seats added. "The best we can do here," Spak told the arrivals. "Four-horse carriages stop at Aranos." They all climbed in and found themselves seats, with the exception of Moon, who stood on a small platform at the rear of the tractor. Kort squeezed into the second car opposite Taya. A couple of Azureans hitching a ride hung on behind. Evidently, formality didn't count for much out here at Icebowl.

"How far out from the Rig have you got now?" Vaysi asked Spak as the short train pulled away and entered the tunnel mouth.

"Just coming up to two miles," Spak replied. Taya

had heard that said over lunch. That was how far they would be going from where they were right now. She tried not to think about it too hard.

The lights strung along the tunnel roof paraded overhead endlessly. At intervals the cars passed other tractor trains coming the other way filled with rock and sand, and groups of Azureans in hard hats and coveralls or native garb. Taya's awareness of the surroundings and the talk going on around her slowly receded, and she spoke not at all. As they traveled back inland, under the bay and the headland, and beneath the icefield beyond, she became lost in a feeling of detachment, as if a part of her mind were disconnecting from the present and slipping back to hear echoes of another time. This was not the first time. She was familiar now with these images that seemed to form of themselves, entering her mind from somewhere beyond the facade presented by the senses.

It was nothing resembling a compelling force, overwhelming her, in the way that Azurean fables sometimes described. More, she became gradually aware of something elusive yet insistent at the back of her thoughts, that she had to focus on to hold. Somehow she became conscious of moving lower beneath first the seabed with the water above, then solid rock, and then the ice above that; and as the feeling grew of being more tightly wrapped in time, a thread of sensations seemed to weave its way down through the layers of her mind, echoing associations all around her as the tunnel penetrated deeper and at the same time farther back into the past.

She didn't pretend to understand these flashes that felt like some kind of insight, but which she had never been able to unravel into anything comprehensible. They could occur randomly and unpredictably when she was surrounded by people; or, as in the present instance, some stimulus might restructure her perceptual world in dimensions that arose internally instead of reflecting the sensory immediacy outside; and then at other times they would steal up on her when she was in solitude and had retreated into the silence of her thoughts. Several of the other Primaries, too, had reported similar experiences, but only in the last few years. Notable among them was Nyelise, who had always been withdrawn and introspective. Possibly that was why she had remained close to Taya.

Mystic claimed that this was another example of biological minds being able to see into the world that lay beyond the material, which was what he had been saying all along. And the other Mecminds— not counting Skeptic, naturally—thought that perhaps there might be something to it. There could be no denying that Merkon's appearance in the skies and the descent of the Mecs had been described by Azureans long ago with an accuracy that ruled out coincidence. But if Azurean eyes had ever been opened to such a world, they were as surely closed now. Mystic's eager attempts to confirm his theories by intense quizzing of Azureans and study of their religions through the early years after Merkon's arrival had come to nothing. There were those like Serephelio—old and weakening now—called seers, who kept alive the teachings from antiquity and whose belief was unwavering. But as far as could be ascertained, in any meaningful sense—certainly not sufficient to have duplicated the feats of the Ancients—they themselves did not "see."

So were these things that happened to Taya and some of the others related to these apparently lost powers? Nobody knew. Skeptic said they had to allow for the possibility that the unique way in which Taya and the other Star Children had come into being might have made them susceptible to moments of instability that meant nothing, perhaps with a tendency for being triggered by suggestion, and there could be no more to it than that.

However, the notion would certainly be a lot more credible if it turned out that the Ancients had indeed been the Builders of Merkon. And Thinker, for one, was convinced that had to be the case. He insisted that the codes which had shaped the bioforms that had grown on Merkon could only have originated on Azure. The planet's atmosphere and surface conditions were too perfectly suited to Merkonian bioforms' needs; anatomically, Merkonians were identical to Azureans; and then it turned out that Azurean cells carried the same molecular codings. Even so, Skeptic was not fully convinced. Impressive as these facts were, he pointed out, they could still be just manifestations of some higher, more universal ordering principle that Merkonian science as yet did not comprehend. All stars were formed according to the same physics; that didn't mean they had all formed in the same place. Proof would require some definite cultural connection between Azure and Merkon, not just similarities that were natural. That was why untangling the riddle of Azure's past had become so important.

If the civilization of the Ancients had indeed built Merkon, it was surely unthinkable that it would not have spread also to Azure's moon. Nevertheless, observation from Merkon had failed to reveal evidence of an advanced cultural presence as had been anticipated. But there were objects all over the surface that reflected strongly from radio to optical wavelengths. When the demands from all the other activities that had sprung up around Azure finally eased sufficiently to permit it, Coordinator agreed to conducting a survey of the moon's surface physically. The expedition had left only recently in a specially constructed craft devised by Engineer for the purpose, unenclosed and carrying no life support since it was purely a mission for the machines. The moon wasn't at all a place suited to biolife. Conceivably, the Ancients had reached the same conclusion, and that was why there were no signs of a presence there.

"Taya?" She realized with a start that the car had stopped. Spak had climbed out and was looking back at her. "We're here. Aren't you coming with us?"

She blinked, collected her senses back together, and smiled. "Yes . . . of course." He offered a hand, and she climbed down to join the others. Ahead of them, the main tunnel widened into a long gallery stretching away, its roof studded with lights and lined by cables and ducts carrying air from the pumping station beneath the Rig. They had stopped at a place where a smaller side tunnel went off to the left. Moon was still on the tractor, and Vaysi had remained in the other car. She had already seen what was that way, she told Spak, and there were some things she wanted to go over with Moon. They'd wait for the rest of the party where their route rejoined the main tunnel. Karthel and Gorso, who had also seen all this before, decided to stay in the cars too.

Eltry and Nyelise went ahead with Spak into the smaller tunnel. Kort moved closer beside Taya as they followed. "I was watching you back there, while we were in the tunnel," he said in a low voice. "What happened?"

"Oh . . . I just had feelings of things very close, yet far away in time. I don't know how else to describe it."

"What kind of things?"

Taya continued looking ahead as they walked. "Anguish. Terror. Millions of voices. . . . Death."

"Did you . . . see anything as well?"

"No. Just feelings. But they were real. People who once lived here felt them."

Kort fell silent for a moment. Ahead, Spak was explaining something to Eltry and Nyelise. "Skeptic has some questions he'd like you to answer," Kort said.

"Tell him, later," Taya sighed. She was having to fight down a feeling of growing claustrophobia as they entered the narrowing passage. The awareness of the distance they had come was weighing on her; that the long tunnel back to the Rig was the only way out. And this was only the beginning.

They came to another long gallery, narrower than the one they had left the cars in, running in roughly the same direction. It followed a run of pipes and tubes, some several feet in diameter, lying in parallel banks below the roped ledge onto which the party had emerged. They continued for some distance, past old and encrusted joints, junctions, flanges, and support mountings. In some places sections were broken, revealing the corroded metal inside. At intervals the lines passed through undisturbed rock, left as roof supports; elsewhere, clean-cut ends and pits hollowed beneath the tubes showed where portions, perhaps containing the remains of pumps or other devices, had been removed. It all had a dank oppressive air, even with the tunnel lights. Taya had the feeling of coming up underneath a graveyard.

"The sublevels of Vrent," Spak said, halting and gesturing after they had come far enough to get a general impression. "These were the lines that handled services like water, power, communications, sewage—

and more that we haven't figured out yet. These are some of the better-preserved parts. In most places, everything was crushed out of recognition. In this general area where we're at, the lower levels filled with mud that hardened enough to offset the pressure."

Nyelise was looking around, only half listening. She drew nearer to Taya, and Taya noticed her shiver. She wondered if Nyelise was being affected in the same kind of way that she was. Kort had no questions. Whatever was known to any Mecmind was available to all of them.

Farther on, the tunnel widened—again to the left. Spak led them to a wide shaft leading down. Inside the shaft was a cable-operated hoist made of wood, and descending beside it a series of ladders and connecting platforms, also of wood. Even with all Engineer's new technologies, wood was still used preferentially wherever practicable. It reduced demands for processed materials, and put to good use the ready supply of Azurean skills and labor.

They boarded the hoist and were lowered down the shaft to a space from which two tunnels ran in opposite directions. . . . At least, Taya first took them to be two tunnels. But then she realized that they were in fact the same tunnel, which the shaft from above had broken into. However, it was completely unlike the gallery they had been following above. That had been more a series of connected excavations, roughly cut, widening and narrowing irregularly, cluttered with props and shoring. The one she found herself looking

173

along now, by contrast, was a *tunnel*. It ran smooth and undeviating inside circular ribbed walls, converging away in one direction until it disappeared from sight in a curve; in the other, running perhaps several hundred yards to an obstruction that looked like the result of a collapse. The floor carried massive rails supported at chest height, surely as thick as the structural beams in Merkon. Taya looked at Spak questioningly.

"One of the transportation systems of the Ancients," he said. "Archaeologist is finding bits of tubes like this all over Azure. We think there might have been a whole planetary net. The base and walls contain a huge electrical system that was probably superconducting." He looked at Nyelise. "Like the transit capsules in Merkon, but on a much bigger scale."

"Were they for carrying people, or moving freight?" Nyelise asked.

"Oh, probably both." Spak pointed in the direction where the tunnel curved out of view. "Farther along that way are the ruins of what was a terminal and access system down to it. We're only just starting to dig it out. Everything was buried in mud and rock there, but it came in from the other direction and didn't penetrate this far."

"Were there . . . people there?" Taya asked.

Spak nodded somberly. "Oh yes. Bones, anyway. Lots of them. Not just people—animals as well"

"Animals?"

"Heaped up to the ceilings, along with smashed up trees, all kinds of things. They must have been washed down in torrents."

Nyelise shuddered again.

Taya frowned. "You mean domestic animals like the Azureans use? But if the Ancients' cities were anything like Merkon, why would they have needed them?"

Spak shook his head. "According to Biologist, bears, deer, buffalo—we're talking about all kinds. There are also some that, if they still exist at all anywhere, we've never seen. And the Azureans don't recognize them either."

Taya's puzzlement increased. "Bears? Buffalo? . . . But animals like those don't live anywhere near here. How could they? The climate's all wrong. Nothing grows here. What would they live on?"

"Our guess is that the floods must have carried them here," Spak said, shrugging.

Taya gave him a pained look. "What, halfway around the planet?" She looked at Kort. "Surely not. I can't believe that."

"And she's not even Skeptic," Eltry said.

Kort rubbed his chin between a steel finger and thumb, and raised his head as if pondering. Lacking facial expression, the Mecs relied heavily on mannerism and gesture. "Well, as it so happens, Skeptic doesn't think so either," he told them.

"So does he have any better ideas?" Spak invited.

"He says that's not his department," Kort returned.

"All right, then. How about Thinker?"

There was another short delay. Then Kort said, "There is another possibility that Thinker and Skeptic have been debating. They weren't going to mention it until they'd explored it a bit more with Scientist. Thinker says maybe such animals once lived a lot closer to these regions. Then they wouldn't have to have been carried over improbable distances."

Spak didn't look convinced. "But how could they have lived closer? Taya's right. The climate could never support them. Nothing grows here."

Kort pointed upward. "And there's ice above us hundreds of feet thick. Who would want to build a city here either?"

Eltry frowned from one to the other. "So what are you saying?" he asked. "That the whole climate changed?"

Kort nodded. "Maybe just that. Scientist agrees that it fits all the facts."

Eltry spread his hands. "But how could it?"

"The only thing that Thinker can think of is that the poles must have shifted somehow," Kort replied.

Vaysi and the others were waiting by the tractor and its two cars in a space where the main gallery ended. Several other passageways led away in different directions, and a shaft led up. Another Mec was standing with them, whose coveralls with their design of yellow and green circles signified to be one of the Archaeologists.

So far there had been little activity to see. This

was no doubt because the workings they had traveled through went back to the earliest probings, and not much new was going on in them. Here, however, the sounds of running machinery and tools in use came from all sides. Another tractor was moving a car filled with rock off one of the hoists from above, while others came and went, hauling loads along the various tunnels. In an alcove housing what looked like water pumps and a compressor, some human figures sitting on a stack of timbers were eating lunch. Closer up, Taya saw from his arm patch that the Archaeologist was the one designated Spade.

"Shop talk," Vaysi said to the arrivals as the two groups joined. "There's a lot being discovered about the rocks that interests me."

"The work going on down at this level and below is mainly archaeological," Spak told Taya. "There were older cities on the site before Vrent was built. But we go up from here, to where it gets more interesting."

The reunited group left Spade to return to whatever task he had been involved in, and ascended a succession of sloping ramps and landings to another working chamber and intersection of more tunnels. Despite the huge fans, the place was oppressively humid and hot, as Spak had warned. Taya tried not to imagine what it would have been like had they kept their outer clothes on.

They crossed a bridge over a chasm with water below, to a cavern cut through solidified rock and debris. On the far side, a constricted section continued beyond an opening topped by an arch of smooth, white material bent into a standing U. Spak pointed to it and told them it was a whale's jawbone, uncovered not ten yards away.

"How on earth did it get down here?" Taya asked, mystified.

"Well, one thing's sure—it didn't swim," Spak answered.

The passage opened into a space bounded on two sides by plane surfaces of clearly artificial origin— old and crumbling walls, sometimes difficult to distinguish from rock that had been incompletely cut away. Glistening wet in parts, they extended upward past the lights into gloom, where the roof above was dark and formless, like a cave's. Holes had been bored at intervals, presumably for materials samples, some of them revealing parts of internal strengthening bars, rusted and corroded. A circular formation five feet or so across marked what had once been some kind of pipe, long rotted into the rock that filled it. Spak told them they were down among the foundations, the roots from which the most recent version of Vrent had sprung.

"I don't see any stones," Nyelise remarked, looking along the walls. All of the older Azurean constructions were built from stone or brick.

"It was molded," Engineer said. "The Ancients made a kind of pourable rock—like the mortar that Azureans use, but more liquid, yet it set harder. We're experimenting with the idea."

"How long have these walls been here?" Taya asked. Something about their mute, brooding solidity made her apprehensive.

"From their carbon content, the bones and other organic substances are at least two thousand years old," Engineer replied. "So the city goes back farther than that."

Two thousand. Taya could remember when she had thought ten years an eternity to wait. And in the layers below, there were remains of older cities still?

A hole blasted through the base of one of the walls brought them to more foundations, this time burst by an ingress of what could have been mud or a finger of lava penetrating from above. Taya registered a series of impressions as they passed through: a massive supporting pier, canted and shifted crazily off its base; everything the other side of it collapsed and compressed under immense weight bearing down from above; mecroids emerging from muddy tunnels like troglodytes of Azurean folk tales. Finally, a tube-frame staircase contained in the scaffolding erected around another hoist took them up another level.

Here, for the first time, they walked across exposed portions of what had evidently been a floor. The space they had ascended into had been largely cleared to reveal a vault recognizably rectangular in all directions. Standing at the near end were the rusted and flaking shapes of what Taya could only

James P. Hogan

think to describe as fossil machines, their original lines barely discernible, some not even fully dug out of the rock that had entombed them. The far end of the hall, however, seemed to have escaped being buried. The lines of the walls there were cleaner, and the machines that remained—spaces told of several having been removed—disintegrating but free of foreign encrustations. Taya moved after the others, staring at these relics from a lost age, trying to picture this place as it once had been: humming, throbbing, and gleaming—like parts of Merkon.

She came to a stop, arrested by the image. Even without sharp lines and color, she was sure that she could make out the same general forms that she had known since childhood. Couldn't the rusting frames standing by the far wall almost have been bulkier versions of the racking inside electronic-photonics cabinets? And weren't those casings with the remains of shafts still protruding virtually the same shape as the motors that Engineer had contrived to propel the *caloosh*? Even as she looked, the strips and remnants of distorted metal laid out on the floor started to take on identifiable shapes as pieces of ducting, conduit, cable. She realized that Spak was watching her and smiling faintly.

"Yes, I know, what you're thinking," he said. "Doesn't it show that the same people built Merkon? We thought the same thing. But Skeptic says anyone would build machines the same basic way."

Taya's bubble popped into soap drops. "Sometimes I think I could happily delete Skeptic and all his backups," she sighed.

"You probably wouldn't be here without him," Spak reminded her. "None of us would."

"That's true, I guess," she conceded. "Okay, I take it back."

"It's all right. I didn't pass it on," Kort told her. "If it's any consolation, Mystic agrees with you."

Spak came back a few paces to stand by her. "But you're close," he said. "There are other machines in better condition that we only found recently. They carry metal tags, which on X-ray examination show impressions that we think were numerals. The forms are uncannily like shapes that are found stamped into structural members in the original parts of Merkon. Even Skeptic agrees that *those* are *not* something that anyone would invent the same way." He gave Taya a moment to absorb that; then he added in a tone that came through immediately as forced nonchalance, "As a matter of fact, that was what gave us the first real clue."

Taya caught the meaningful look in his eye. "First?" she repeated. Excitement seized her. "There's more? Are you saying you're sure?"

The twitching of Spak's mouth broadened into a smile that he could no longer contain. "Yes, of course, Taya. We have some big news. You don't think we'd bring you all this way just to show you a few walls and rusty pipes, do you?"

Taya turned accusingly to Kort. "You knew, didn't you! Even before we left Aranos."

"They made me promise," Kort protested. He threw his hands up helplessly. "Human children. . . . What do you do?"

"We are not!" Vaysi told him.

"You're all impossible to argue with, anyway," Kort said.

"Never mind all that," Taya told them. Then, to Spak, "Tell me what you've found."

"Just a few more minutes, and we'll show you," he replied.

They returned to the scaffolding and stairs, but boarded the hoist this time. It was larger than the one they had used back in the tunnel, able to hold several cars at a time. For perhaps thirty or forty feet they ascended past galleries that had been opened to expose more sections of walls and floors; then came part of a vertical shaft and a stairway that were not newly formed but had been part of the original structure. Then the hoist emerged abruptly into a high, open space, the largest they had seen so far, and stopped.

Taya stepped off the platform with Kort, behind the others; a mecroid that had been waiting began trundling the first four of a line of loaded cars onto the vacated hoist.

Unlike the gray, stonelike floors below, the surface here had consisted of glazed mosaics—reminiscent of the ornamentation in some of the grander buildings around Azure today, such as Cyron's former palace at Aranos. Although much of the tiling was gone, patches remained where the rock had been painstakingly removed to reveal recognizable designs, in some places with vestiges of the original colors. As Taya took in more of the surroundings, the components came together in her mind's eye to recreate something of the scene as it must have existed.

The broad steps to the right had been part of a curving stairway to a terrace above, the overlooking balustrade of which still stood. To the left, the oval depression and piles of displaced blocks that looked as if they had formed a wall around it had been some kind of pool. The partly reconstructed sculpture on one side had stood on the pedestal island. Above and beyond the terrace, four square columns framed what had been a portico through the wall standing behind. The immense rectangular openings through it had held windows.

Taya indicated the wall to Spak and looked up at it again. "The building that that belonged to," she said. "Are we inside it or outside?"

"Outside. We've come out from what were service levels below into some kind of ornamental plaza, maybe a garden or small park."

Taya looked up. The space above narrowed as it got higher, like an inverted canyon, one side formed by the exposed facade of the building, the other cut away into terraces and ramps by exploratory teams pursuing various goals. Horizontal struts had been thrown across the gap to shore up the exposed wall as more of its supporting matrix was dug away. Amid scaffolding to one side, the shape of what could have been a bridge or arch was beginning to emerge. Mixed groups of human figures and both wheeled and legged mecroids were busy at varied tasks, shoveling, scraping, washing down exposed surfaces with water. A crew higher up were positioning a drill. On an improvised table, a mecform that looked like another version of Archaeologist was drawing on a chart.

She turned to look in the other direction.

The upside-down canyon ended at an excavated cliff of rock layers showing the sequence of Vrent's engulfment, which Taya was already familiar with from the accounts she had heard and read. First were the darker bands below, like those they had been ascending through, formed from compacted sediments and mud. Above them, a thinner layer, ten feet or so thick, of sand and clays. Finally, above that, the lighter grays of lava that extended to the surface. There had been extensive lava flows all over Azure following the flooding. Presumably, some connection with the Conflagration was implied.

Taya shielded her eyes with a hand against the glare from the lights, trying vainly to make out the roof. "How high does this go?" she asked Vaysi.

"Let's see . . . the last time I was here, the excavation itself went up about fifty or sixty feet, with pilot shafts above that following the building for about the same distance again." Vaysi called to Spak. "Hey,

Spak. How far up have you gone with the pilot tubes now?"

"We broke through to the ice about two days ago," he replied.

"To the ice?" Vaysi looked surprised. "But that has to be over four hundred feet."

"Right." Spak gave a satisfied nod, as if she ought to be impressed. He added, before she could ask, "Yep, the building's still there, all the way. It just keeps going."

"Four hundred feet!" Taya repeated, astonished. No Azurean architecture came near to such a height.

"And there was more to it above that," Spak said.

Moon, who had been surveying the various works in progress and saying little, explained, "What didn't get washed away in the flooding was set solid in the lava. Then the top parts were sliced off and carried away by the ice—which is how the things in the bergs came to be there. We'll possibly never know for sure how much was lost above the ice."

News of the Star Mother's coming had evidently been telegraphed ahead. As Taya and the others climbed the wooden stairs that had been erected over the partly missing original flight, and emerged into view on the terrace, figures all around stopped what they were doing to turn and look at her. Here and there some raised a hand. She waved back in acknowledgement.

Between the square columns, the entrance into the building could now be seen, shored up by steel props.

In front of it, a collection of trophies had been assembled of articles recovered from the workings. More Azureans approached and stood watching curiously as Spak, Moon, and others from the party described some of the exhibits to Taya.

There were several human skeletons, assembled on wire supports. An array of items set out in trays included metal clasps and buckles from clothing, assorted pieces of jewelry, hammers, saws, handles, as well as bits and rods that Moon said came from other tools. There were eating and kitchen implements; more remains of mechanisms and electronics devices, purposes not identified; shards of ornaments and glassware. Moon said that the Ancients used glass extensively in their buildings, the weight of the structure being carried by internal piers. That was why so much of the wall was missing, and the remains of the entrance just a shell. One of the skeletons was intriguing. It was fitted with an artificially constructed hip joint, beautifully fashioned from metal. Replacing parts in that way was something that had never occurred to Medic. But that could have been just because he had only dealt with biopeople who were young. Many Azureans complained of painful and stiffening joints as they got older.

By the time the group moved on into the building itself, a small entourage had collected and followed them. The vestibule area had been excavated only enough to reveal its general shape and dimensions. A partly opened arch beyond led to what seemed to be a circular space, the floor on the far side elevated to form a shelf from which borings radiated in several directions like fingers probing to find the limits of the space they were in. Nothing extensive had been uncovered or connected up. In this direction was an exposed wall; up that way, a part of something high and horizontal; off to one side, an opening into a shaft that Engineer thought might have been an elevator. It all had the look of being new and recently uncovered. This was evidently where some of the most current work was going on.

Spak and Vaysi, with Moon, led the way along a passage flanking the shelf toward a brightly lit working area. Eltry drew ahead with them, while Nyelise stayed with Taya and Kort. Gorso and Karthel dropped back among the Azureans still following. More figures were standing in the roughly hewn chamber ahead. Taya got the feeling they had been waiting. Among them she made out another version of Archaeologist—it was Archaeologist Claws, holding a screenpad. Tools and other instruments lay all around and on a work bench rigged from planks and trestles. The roof props still looked temporary, and air was delivered via a hose lying along the floor. Clearly, this was one of the newest places to be dug out. The figures that had been waiting opened to admit the newcomers, and then joined them in forming a semicircle before what had been found there.

It was another sculpture, this time of a human form: the head and shoulders, three feet or so high, of a man—set on a plinth in a partly uncovered recess. But what had obviously been the objects of the most care and attention were the two marble slabs set into the wall on either side of the plinth, and another forming the floor in front of it. They had been cleaned and polished, surely almost to their original condition. The shapes carved into them, set in groups along straight, equispaced lines, were bold and decisive. After studying them for a while, Taya began picking out similarities and repetitions. Eltry moved up to stand beside her. She looked at him, asking an unvoiced question.

"Writing of the Ancients," he confirmed. "Maybe some kind of ceremonial script. They probably had many." Taya was not sure what she was supposed to say.

Archaeologist lifted the pad that he was holding. "You know, of course, how Scientist finally discovered the secret of human DNA coding in data that had been copied and passed down from Merkon's earliest machines?"

Taya nodded. A long time had gone by since Kort first told her that story. She had repeated it many times since to the other Primaries when they were children.

Archaeologist went on, "A lot of the program code that still runs in Merkon today can be traced back to the original machines of the Builders. Included in it are tables of control codes that generate characters on screens." He gestured to indicate the lines carved in the marble slabs. "Three days ago, after we dissolved away the last layers that had been obscuring these, Scientist ran a search of those old tables again. This is what he found."

The pad illuminated to show columns of symbols. Every alternate column consisted of single-character entries that Archaeologist had highlighted in red. Taya looked at them, moved her eyes to scan the forms cut into the marble slabs again, then back. Although many of the shapes on the screen were not represented, there could be no doubt: The characters on the slabs were from the same set.

Spak joined her and Eltry as the meaning sank slowly in. "It's the proof," he said quietly from behind them. "Skeptic is convinced. We've returned to where we originated from, Taya. The Ancients were the Builders of Merkon."

Back on land that evening, Icebowl Base decided it was time to relax and party. Nobody talked about the work at Vrent or theories about the Ancients. In the communal mess area at the center of the score-or-so timber huts and dugouts, surrounded by equipment and supplies, a fowl-and-venison dinner was organized in honor of the Star Mother, with liberal dispensation of Leorican wine, thoughtfully brought up by Vaysi on the flyer for the occasion. Afterward, Eltry juggled and performed balancing acts, Spak entertained with stories from the year that had gone by, the Azureans sang songs and clapped to their traditional instruments, and Archaeologist Claws joined clumpingly in the dancing.

Taya stayed through most of the evening, playing her part and showing appreciation. But although all her formative years had been spent in the confines of Merkon, after the closeness of the tunnels she needed air. As the time drew closer to midnight with no sign of any abatement or slackening of the pace, pleading a long day that had commenced with a flight from far away across Azure, she bade everyone to enjoy the rest of the party and took her leave to return to the quarters that she was sharing with Vaysi and Nyelise in an adjacent hut. Nyelise, who had left earlier, was asleep when Taya got there. Vaysi was still going strong, stamping and whirling through Azurean dances. Taya still needed space and solitude for a while before being shut up again. She hung up her cloak, put on a set of furs that Spak had given her to try, and went back outside.

The sun had dipped below the horizon for the two-hour night, but to the south the moon stood full and white in a sky that had cleared during the day. Beyond the huts and their surrounding litter of vehicles, containers, equipment, and supply dumps, slopes of churned snow rose to a line of rocky bluffs in the inland direction, and more gently to a white ridge on the seaward side. Thrusting her hands deep into the pouches in the front of the fur jacket, Taya turned in the direction of the ridge and made her way through the outer parts of the base to the bottom of the snowfield. The snow beyond was firm, and she found she could move over it fairly easily. She stopped to breathe in the night and experience its intoxication. Then, setting a diagonal course across and up the slope, she resumed walking at a slow, easy pace toward the ridgeline. As she walked, she went through the day's events again, fitting the new pieces in with things known and conjectured previously concerning the strange story that was coming together of Azure's past.

It had been suspected for a long time, but now there could be no doubt: Azure had been the home of the race that built Merkon. The Azureans who existed today were descended from them. And yet, thrown back to conditions of primitiveness and divided into their tribes and nations as they might be, there were those among them who had known. They had known that children from those far-off aeons would one day return accompanied by silver beings from the stars. Scientist couldn't explain it. Skeptic couldn't deny it. How could it be?

It could mean only one thing. In the final, Golden Age that must have represented the culmination of their achievements, before that final calamity, the Ancients had discovered, or had cultivated, or there had somehow arisen, a power of insight that even now none of the intelligences of Merkon could explain, that had been lost. But through traditions passed down through the few like Serephelio, some of the things disclosured in such insights had been preserved. And now Taya, and to a lesser degree several younger ones of her kind, were experiencing these moments of detached perception that seemed to manifest themselves as strange affinities toward that same, mysterious epoch in the past. Was it possible that in a way nobody understood, the circumstances of their origins had recreated in the Star Children a germ of what had once existed, which the cataclysm that befell the home world had extinguished along with all else?

Taya hadn't really registered arriving at the top of the ridge. She became aware of the slope easing off, and then there was nowhere higher to go. The top was wide and rounded. She moved forward until she was looking down the reverse side, falling in a shallow slope toward the line marking the top of the ice cliffs. Beyond lay the sea, rippling silver in the moonlight. A dark finger of land to her right marked the edge of the bay. In the center of the bay, directly ahead as she looked, were the lights of the Rig. The tunnel below it would run back to very near where she stood. She pictured again the city whose remains she had barely caught a glimpse of. How much more of it, even now as she stood there, lay waiting to be discovered, directly beneath her feet?

She felt her mind slipping. . . .

All at once it was as if the ice and the rock were not there, and she were looking down over the immensity of Vrent as it had existed. She saw that everything uncovered in a year of labor was as nothing—the twig confused with the forest; a pebble mistaken for a mountain. For just an instant, in some inversion that kaleidoscoped time and space, she saw the glass canyons of color and light, arches and towers, vehicles streaming on level upon level beneath the teeming terraces and soaring pinnacles . . . And then a sudden intrusion upon her senses from without swept it away as if a light had been turned off.

A mecroid running on sausage-shaped rollers was drawing to a halt behind her in the snow. She turned fully and saw Kort sitting in one of the four plastic seats ahead of the flatbed rear section. "I wondered if your legs were getting stiff in the cold while you were standing up here looking at the sea," he said. "Thought you might appreciate a ride back."

"How did you know I was looking at the sea?" Taya asked.

"I know everything," Kort said.

It was a private joke between them, echoed from long ago. Taya smiled tiredly. "Yes, I would—thanks. But not just yet. It's so quiet and peaceful after all that drilling and banging today. And then the party. How does Vaysi keep going like that? I wonder if growing up on a planet has anything to do with it."

Kort got down from the truck and came around to stand beside her. He was wearing a stretch cap and coverall of dark oilskin. Taya chuckled. "What's funny?" the robot asked.

"The Azureans used to think you were silver gods. You look more like a fisherman who's lost his boat."

"Hm. And I could say that you look like a seal hunter with a cold nose." He meant it literally. Kort could see in the infrared.

A series of sharp cracks sounded from somewhere along the cliff line below, followed by muffled crashes of ice falling into the ocean.

"The Rig looks like Cyron's old palace at night," Taya said. "I wonder if the Ancients had ships like that—all lit up like floating cities. . . . Hasn't all kinds of wreckage been found that Engineer says could have been from huge seagoing vessels?"

"Some of it was a long way from any oceans," Kort reminded her. "Wouldn't it be simpler to assume some specialized kind of land structures that we don't know anything about? Or even crashed flying vehicles."

"The floods could have carried them there," Taya said.

"But some of them were found high up in the mountains. You'd need tidal waves miles high."

"Well, things like whales and tropical trees were found high up in mountains too. How did *they* get there?"

Kort looked up unconsciously at the sky, which often meant he was communicating with Merkon. "Skeptic says he'll believe it when you show him a mechanism capable of producing waves that are miles high," he said.

Taya had no response to that, and fell silent for a while. When she spoke again, her voice was distant and reflective, as if she were half talking to herself.

"I started to see it, just before you came—Vrent, the way it used to be. It was . . . I don't know how you'd describe it. Imagine Merkon opened out and stretched toward the sky. There were bridges and towers, a traffic of people and machines flowing in rivers. . . . Glass mountains of light."

"How can you know it was the way Vrent used to be?" Kort asked.

"I just . . . *know*."

A few seconds passed—enough to convey that Kort had considered the proposition and not seem impolite. "Subjective impressions of biominds are noted for their inventiveness," he pointed out. Taya couldn't suppress a smile. At times the machines' concessions to delicacy could be touching. "The Azurean proclivity for deliberately inducing chemically assisted hallucinations is well known."

"Kort, I haven't been drinking or smoking any of their awful pipes."

"Long, stressful day. Powerful emotional stimuli. Extended period deprived of sleep. . . . All notorious enhancers of autosuggestion," Kort pointed out.

Taya sighed and stared up at the moon. "What about the old prophecies that seers like Serephelio kept alive? Were they autosuggestion? Skeptic has been through the records like a cat picking apart a dead fish, and even he can't deny them. Mystic has just about accepted all the Azurean gods."

"Yes, and we all know Mystic," Kort said. He looked at her and shook his head. "That the Ancients could know things in ways that we don't understand appears to be fact. You and some of the others have occasional experiences that you believe might be related. But that is entirely conjecture. You say you saw the city that was. Well, maybe so, but there's no way it can be verified. It could be pure invention—unconscious and unintentional, maybe, but an invention nevertheless. Now, if any of you could do what the Ancients did and tell us something that *will be* . . ." Kort stopped, seeing that Taya was giving him a reproachful look. "What?"

"Is that you talking, Kort, or Skeptic?" she asked.

"Oh, well, yes, I suppose it was. But he's got a point, you know."

Taya could see that this wasn't going anywhere. "We need to talk with Serephelio again," she declared. "I want to learn more about what he knows. . . . And in the meantime, you're right. It's starting to get cold. Let's get back." Kort nodded. They turned back toward the truck. Taya paused and looked across at him as she was about to climb up. "Don't machine minds ever feel anything like that?" she asked him. "Not even the most tiny, fleeting glimmer?"

"No, never," Kort replied.

Vaysi would be staying on at Icebowl to take a bigger part in the study of Vrent and learn more from the excavations. Taya and Nyelise, with Kort, stayed through the following day, resting and meeting others whose schedules had kept them away previously. It was late evening—though still daylight—when the flyer finally lifted off the pad, got a nav fix and weather update from the satellites launched by Merkon, and set itself a flight plan for Aranos. Eltry was returning too, having spent long enough amid the ice and the remoteness. Several Azureans and a cargo of samples recovered from Vrent filled the rest of the space. Fast transportation was still rare and precious; never a square foot was wasted.

Night came as their course took them southward. After talking for a while initially, Eltry produced his pad and a sheaf of notes to tidy up some work, and Nyelise settled down with a book of epics from a faraway region east of Leorica. The Azureans, luxuriating in the unaccustomed comfort of the cabin and still suffering from the effects of the previous night's party, fell asleep one by one. Kort was perceptually on the moon, sharing experiences from the expedition that Scientist and Engineer had organized there, which meant that he would respond locally if addressed, but otherwise was not initiating conversation. Taya was left with her own thoughts, staring down at cloud forms sailing like ghostly white swans in the darkness on Azure's black ocean below. Samir had told her how he'd thought the first lander to come down from Merkon was a giant swan, she remembered.

Twenty years. It seemed as if that had all been a different world. Well, in a real sense of things that mattered to her, it had been a different world. She remembered her initial bewilderment at the violence and senseless cruelty they had found; how it had turned to disbelief and revulsion in the weeks that followed as the picture unfolded in all its diseased ugliness of whole societies organized for war; her horror at discovering systematic plundering, destruction, the infliction of torture and imprisonment, policies of control through persecution and fear. . . . For a long time after that she had known just numbness. But news was carried from nation to nation of Cyron's return from the dead, and the miracle of how the "Vengeful" had transformed into the "Forgiving." None could deny the invincible gods of silver who had descended, and as time went by, more came to meet the children from the stars, who knew no word for "death," showed the way of gentleness, and had spared even those who had mistreated them. And slowly the peoples of Azure were learning. Much, indeed, had changed.

Taya hadn't noticed its appearance, but she became conscious suddenly of an eerie orange glow filling the sky outside. And yet, even as her awareness expanded to take in the source of the light, another part of her mind knew that she was not turning her head, nor had she even moved in her seat toward the window. It was a cloud of yellow incandescence extending across half the sky, solid at one end, breaking and widening into a flail of twisting knots and filaments. As if in a dream, she found herself perceiving it from different perspectives simultaneously: against stars seen from where three silver domes and a tower stood amid plains of gray rock; and as an apparition flaming in the day skies of what she knew was Azure even as she felt the terror of those who had watched it. The walls of the cabin, the aircraft, the moment of time that she was in dissolved out of existence as she beheld not just the part of Azure below but its whole surface combined in a superposition of images. She saw from above the green plateaus of water advancing across continents at the same time as she stared up, petrified from the cities being washed away and disappearing under mountainous walls of surging white; she saw the earth opening up in rifts that tore across mountains and ocean, vomiting fire and lavas, landscapes upended, seas emptied and boiling; she felt the winds that plucked forests from the ground, the stones that fell like rain while lightning crashed in continual sheets. And then came the dark that lasted years, broken only by the death glow of a world aflame. The darkness became the black sky of stars again; the gray rock beneath had become a molten river pouring over, inside, and around, covering the ruins of the three silver domes and the fallen tower.

Taya realized that the sound of the engines had stopped. They were on the ground. She blinked, shook her head, and looked out. It was daylight at the landing ground behind what had once been the prison at Aranos.

"Kort, I think she's waking up," a voice called out. It was Nyelise's. She was sitting across the cabin, eating a snack of bread with cheese and pickles, and drinking tea. She had set another dish aside for Taya. The sound came of feet clambering up steps to the flyer, and Kort appeared in the doorway moments later.

"So you're back with us?" he said, looking at Taya. She nodded, still struggling to accommodate. In some ways the vision still felt more real. "How do you feel?" Kort asked.

Finally, Taya shook away the last wisps of what she had seen, and recomposed herself. "Hungry," she answered. Nyelise handed her the dish and turned to fill another mug from the tea jug.

"I never saw you so enraptured before," Kort said. "We thought it best to leave you be."

It was three days later when they arrived at Serephelio's cottage, Taya riding a gray mare, Kort striding alongside and keeping up easily at walking pace. Nobody had ever been able to persuade Serephelio to keep a screenpad in the house. Mecroids and electricity were too much. When Cyron died—permanently this time—having long ago become Serephelio's steady companion for philosophic discussions and card playing far into the night, Serephelio had left the city and found a less complicated place to live on the edge of a forest just outside a village to the south of Aranos.

They prepared a dinner of vegetables from the garden, fish from the lake a mile through the forest, and a leg of lamb left by one of the villagers as a gift. Then Serephelio opened a bottle of cognac and settled down with his pipe, while his dog, Narzin, named after the King's champion of old, dozed in front of the hearth. Taya and Kort told him of the latest findings at Vrent. They summarized their discussions since and gave Skeptic's views. Finally, Taya described her most recent experience during the flight back to Aranos.

Serephelio listened attentively, studying her face from time to time but interrupting little while he puffed clouds of blue smoke into the air. Although his face seemed shriveled with lines now, and his hair and beard were white, his gray eyes were still alert and bright. In his presence, Taya always got the feeling that he knew more than he admitted to.

"In truth, 'tis all as was written long ago, before any of the nations that exist today were known or their tongues even spoke," he told them when she had finished. He quoted a translation that she had heard many times. *"Medila, the goddess who brings retribution with many arms, came down in wrath upon the world.* Could not this burning object in the sky of which you speak have appeared as a many-armed creature wielding swords, which legends of many peoples relate?"

Taya nodded. "Or at least, have been interpreted that way by people who didn't understand what the original terms meant." People who came later, who had lost their knowledge of astronomy, could have read descriptions of celestial events to be clashes between deities.

201

"The same is told all over Azure," Serephelio said. "First the floods: mountains of water swept over the lowlands and through the valleys. In some places only the mountaintops were untouched. Then the earth shaking and rending, venting its fires. He quoted again: *And the beasts of the earth fled. In great numbers they did run in terror, but sanctuary there was none. And the forests did turn to ash and the seas to deserts.*" He relit his pipe with a spill from the fire. "All as you described. Lightning and thunderbolts unending, the survivors perishing beneath torrents of hot rocks that fell from the heavens. Then came the rains that quenched the fires, and afterward the snows. The lands covered by ice, and darkness endured for years. And when it lifted, the directions of the rising and the setting sun, and the courses of the stars, had changed."

Taya looked at Kort. "There's the polar shift that Thinker said might have occurred. Wouldn't something huge that almost collided with Azure do all that? And if it was highly electric, couldn't huge sparks jumping across between it and Azure give you all that lightning?"

Kort shuffled his legs. Narzin opened an eye suspiciously. He still hadn't quite accepted this metal figure in his territory, whose odors were all wrong. "The problem is, you were familiar with all the Azurean legends before," Kort pointed out. "And you learned only a few days ago about Thinker's wondering if the poles had shifted. It could all have been incorporated into something that your mind created. Not deliberately, of course. I'm just saying—well, all right, Skeptic is—that we can't rule it out."

"What about the domes and the tower?" Taya said. "I couldn't have incorporated those, because I've never seen them."

"Exactly, and that's the problem," Kort replied. "Neither has anyone else."

"It was nighttime . . . somewhere in mountains," Taya persisted.

"But there's nothing to back it up. None of the things that do have any kind of independent corroboration are new. And the only thing that is original could be a biomind invention." Kort spread his hands.

Taya thought around for a different approach, some item she might have missed, but there were none. The same debate that they had been through on the ice ridge above Icebowl would only repeat itself. She sighed, nodded in resignation, and sat back in her chair, staring at the fire.

Serephelio had listened to these exchanges before and knew that no questions were going to be settled tonight. "It seems our vessel of discovery is aground on sands of conjecture," he observed. "Allow me, then, to beach alongside it a different craft of my own constructing. Thus, leastwise we can entertain each other while we await together the tide of evidence that will float us off."

"You mean a different theory about what happened to the Ancients?" Taya said.

The seer shook his head. "No, enough has been

said of that. A surmising not of what brought about their end, but of what their end brought about. 'Twas not just the Ancients who were fallen, but all humanity from a perfection that was meant to be, and which had all but been achieved."

Taya frowned. "I'm not sure I understand."

"Nor am I, but continue," Kort said, staring fixedly.

"You say it is proved that the Star Children were of Azure born," Serephelio said.

"The facts seem to point that way pretty conclusively," Kort agreed.

"Aye, the evidence that your system insists on finally attests, whereas I myself have never doubted it." Serephelio raised a hand. "I don't claim to understand it, mind you, for I am told that Merkon was beyond the circles of stars." He shrugged. "But so many of your mysteries lie as far beyond the circle of my understanding that adding this as well makes no difference that I would quarrel over." He looked at them for a second, then took a drink while he retraced his thread.

"Before the Cataclysm, Azure had reached an age of splendor that possibly even Star Children are unable to imagine. These methods that you call science had given its people mastery of the material world. They could create wealth without limit out of rock, through the power that lies locked in matter. They could cross the world in an hour, talk with any person anywhere, and view distant events as they happened. They built cities in the sky, and voyaged in them out among the stars. This much I know more from what you have told than from anything that my own studies on Azure have ever revealed." Serephelio paused and looked at Taya pointedly.

"But it is my belief that the Ancients achieved more than just this. Besides mastering the secrets of the physical world, they also mastered themselves. They learned to free their minds of the hatreds and jealousies, fear and greed that had reduced Azure to what it had become twenty years ago when you arrived. And in that process their minds were awakened to become capable of insights to truth in ways that we have never known. . . . *That* was the true loss that was suffered with the fall of the Ancients."

This was so close to what Taya herself had thought many times that she felt herself getting visibly excited. "It *has* to be so," she said, turning her head appealingly toward Kort. "The things that were predicted. . . . They *knew*. Those can't be just coincidences. Even Scientist agrees."

Kort stared at her for a second, then shifted his gaze to Serephelio, rubbing his chin to indicate reservations. "This isn't a different boat that you've arrived in at all, is it," he said. "It's really another way of supporting Taya's claims. In arguing for the reality of this power of the Ancients, you're suggesting that not quite all of it was lost—that a spark was preserved in the beings that were recreated in Merkon."

Serephelio stared back unwaveringly and nodded. "Very well, so you see through my disguise. But why shouldn't it be so? Have you not confirmed to me this very night that the Ancients were their true progenitors?"

Kort seemed to think for a second. "Only in the sense that they were both formed by the same genetic codes. What you're saying would mean that this ability somehow resides in certain genetic combinations. All Scientist did was find out how to express the codes. If they contained this power that you're talking about, shouldn't it be even more in evidence here on Azure? If several instances arose among the fewer than fifty individuals that were created on Merkon, then in a population of millions of Azureans . . ." Kort stopped as he saw that Serephelio was already shaking his head.

"The *potential* was there," Serephelio said. "But potential is does not always become the reality. The potential for the tree is in the seed; but 'expressing' it—to use your own term—requires earth, water, and sunlight.

"The Ancients not only created the means of producing unlimited wealth; they used that wealth wisely. They used it to free their lives from the want and toil that had kept them functioning at a brute level of existence, little removed from the animal—or perhaps it was the release from want that enabled them to become wise. Either way, the result was the same: They discovered the way to achieve peace in

206

themselves and with the universe. And that was the earth and the water and the sunlight that the seed needed to put out roots and grow."

Taya could see the analogy in its completeness now. "That's what you're telling us was really lost here on Azure," she said. "The potential never disappeared."

"Why should it? The . . ." Serephelio glanced questioningly at Kort.

"Codes," Kort supplied.

". . . the codes were still the same."

Taya went on, "But after the Cataclysm, the conditions for expressing it no longer existed."

Serephelio nodded. "Nothing mattered beyond survival," he said solemnly. "There was total reversion to the level of the beast. Those who learned to kill and to take, without mercy or compassion, would maybe live to see the sun again—some of them. Giving quarter to the woman or children of another was to rob the food from one's own. And by this law was fashioned the Azure to which you returned."

There was no need for him to spell out the rest, or for Taya to comment. Did any other vestige of the civilization of the Ancients still exist out there among the stars in some shape or form? There was no way of telling. But in one tiny speck of the universe at least, the life that Azure had once known in all its fullness had been revived again, and had come home.

Serephelio concluded, "But that which once was has been returned to us, and the world is learning again the ways of wisdom and gentleness. All that Azure became shall flourish one day again."

Kort interlaced his fingers, studied them, and looked up after a respectful silence. "Fine sailing words. But your boat is still beached," he pointed out.

"Bah!" Serephelio waved a hand. "I weary of sitting in grounded boats. Join me and soar with the birds."

"How should I do that?" Kort asked.

"Believe what I say and share the wonder of it."

"But how can I? What evidence do I have that what you say is true?"

Serephelio pointed a finger at Taya. "The evidence is sitting there, right next to you," he said.

Not unexpectedly, the expedition sent by the machines to Azure's moon turned up more new questions than it answered. The first was that of the moon's origin. The surface composition was of a very different mix from Azure's rocks, and doubts immediately sprang up as to whether the two bodies had even formed in the same region of the Vaxis system. Thinker advanced one possibility after another, all of which were promptly holed by Scientist or Skeptic, and so far the issue wasn't even close to being resolved.

A question that the endeavor did settle was that the moon had indeed been disturbed massively in recent times. Thermal gradients in the surface layers, seismic and volcanic activity—all were consistent with such a notion, but not conclusive since they could equally have been the result of radioactive heat sources in the interior. It was the evidence of widespread lava flows and intensive meteorite bombardment in comparatively recent times that decided it. How was it known that these events took place recently? From the remains of the advanced civilization that had existed there and been obliterated, which were scattered all over the surface. Those, of course, were the sources of the radio and radar reflections that had attracted the machines' attention and aroused their curiosity in the first place.

And that was where the three domes and the tower were eventually discovered four months later. They were as Taya had described: broken and pounded under the meteorite storm, the remains almost completely buried in solidified lava. The black sky and the stars that she had seen had been part of a moonscape, not nighttime in any part of Azure at all.

Serephelio died the following year, satisfied and content, although no answer had yet been offered to the final question of what had brought about the Cataclysm.

The first comet to be observed since Merkon's arrival at Vaxis appeared in the outer parts of the star's planetary system six months later. Although considerably smaller than the body estimated to have ended the civilization of the Ancients, it possessed all the necessary characteristics: It was volatile, breaking up into an incandescent halo and streamers of rock and gas as it approached the sun; it was massive, with a high metallic content; it was enormously energetic electrically. Scientist calculated that a similar object large enough to have caused the gravitational upheavals recorded across Azure and its moon could have generated enough heat through eddy-currents induced in the planet's iron- and nickel-bearing rocks to evaporate the oceans to a depth of hundreds of feet. Rapid cooling following the absorption of dust into Azure's atmosphere would account for the massive precipitation as rain and snow, and the ensuing ice cover. Although Serephelio never lived to see the comet, at Taya's insistence it was named after him.

Nyelise and Eltry were married soon afterward, before it had faded from the night sky.

Kort, after much thought, reflection, and talking with Taya, extended his composite personality to incorporate parts of Mystic along with the others. There could be, he told Skeptic, no arguing with the evidence.

THE STILLNESS AMONG THE STARS

1

Cyron's former palace had dominated the center of an Aranos that had witnessed ritual mass killings to appease wrathful gods, and staged death duels between prisoners as a spectacle to entertain the public. Now it was preserved as a museum to an age that was distant, yet needed not to be forgotten. Its spires, once the first part of the city to be seen by a traveler approaching from any direction, had been absorbed into the skyline of metal-ribbed domes and glass-faced towers rising around it. Immediately to the west stood the *Scalitryum* with its marbled arcades and long, stepped terraces—a combination of university and what in bygone times would have been called a temple, devoted to the study and celebration of "Vivance," best described as a mingling of science and an intuitive belief system dealing with the common creativity exhibited by Mind and Life. On the far side was the administrative center for the area's water, electricity, and sewage-disposal services. A theater hall and school of drama had been built beyond that, where the old prison had once been, and next to it was a residential tower topped by a TV studio and communications antennas.

Taya's residence lay about a mile north of the central district, in an area still consisting mainly of individual homes and apartment settings scattered amid greenery and trees. Once the town villa of a leather-and-fabrics-importing family who had migrated to tropical regions, it dated from the second decade after the "Advent," as Merkon's arrival had come to be known, and from which official dates were reckoned. It was spacious yet modest in style, as suited her taste, and at the same time sufficiently secluded, without being remote, to keep from being intrusive the flow of the devout, the curious, and others, who still came out in the course of a visit to the capital with the hope of glimpsing the Sky Mother, or perhaps just to stand for a while and contemplate, nourishing their spiritual affinity with the sense of physical closeness to her abode. In addition to her personal living space, the villa had been refurbished to include quarters for guests and the staff she had gathered to assist her through her ailing years. Also, there were several rooms that had been set aside for receiving the visitors and consultants that had passed through over the years. Far from abating as the Star Children grew older ("Primaries" was no longer used; the Azurean term for them had become generally adopted), her role as counselor and advice giver had expanded until at times it seemed she had become a mentor to the whole planet. But as Taya felt the need to give more of her time to solitude and rest, those activities had reduced to a minimum. These days, only one of the reception rooms was used, and her appearances in public were confined to special or symbolic occasions.

Many Azureans, particularly among the elders whose beliefs remained rooted in the older traditions, still regarded her as the incarnation of a supernatural being. None of the Mecminds, despite their mastery of the physical world and ability to explain in detail how the first of the Star Children had come into being, had seen fit to tell them they were wrong. How could they? For while it was one thing to be able to list the codes that had turned Scientist's first speck of life into a being that grew and thought, they had no more idea where those codes had come from than they had of how the codes had come together that directed the assemblies of the birds and flowers on Azure.

Nothing had changed much in that respect since the earliest days, Kort reflected as he tuned in idly to the current dispute going on between Mystic and Skeptic, with intermittent input from Thinker, Biologist, and Evolutionist. Kort wasn't contributing anything himself. The debate went around and around the same circles endlessly, and he was weary of it. Sometimes he thought that perhaps the more traditional of the Azureans had the right idea: Make up your mind once and for all what you believe, and let that be an end to it. Even as he thought it, the part of him that was drawn from Mystic applauded while the Scientist part writhed in protest. Being the most composite of all the Mecminds might have an advantage in flexibility, but he had long ago learned that another side to it was the inability ever to be absolutely sure of anything. But that could also have its benefits in that it gave him more time to think instead of getting embroiled in interminable, single-viewpoint arguments that never went anywhere. That also applied to Thinker, of course, for being able to formulate any point of view was Thinker's nature. But that very fact made him incapable of adopting any opinion on anything in preference to another, so decisions always ended up being taken by the others.

There were times when Kort felt that he had more in common with the humans of both kinds— Merkonian and Azurean. They seemed to function as composites of fragmented mentalities too, that were constantly in conflict or alliance among themselves, one seemingly gaining control one day, and at some other time another. Psychologist thought that was what gave them their colorful and volatile personalities. The Mecminds had their personalities too, but in a way that was more predictable. When Skeptic, Mystic, and Scientist, for example, became involved in an argument, it was generally easy to anticipate the line that each would take, and they never deviated from it. With humans, you could never tell. It all depended which one of the persons in their head was in charge. Sometimes the other

Mecminds told Kort that he baffled them in the same way.

An interrupt from one of the house sensors told Kort that Irbane had come out of Taya's private suite and was heading toward the library, where Kort was scanning the morning's outgoing mail and forwarding it to the local Azurenet link node. Technically it would have been possible for Kort to have followed the proceedings with the visitors inside with Taya, but through habit and courtesy, Kort observed the conventional respect for privacy. From the hunched strain of the young man's gait and the tension written into the muscles of his face, Kort read that Irbane was troubled.

Having dispatched the mail, Kort directed the received messages that he was holding for Taya through to her notepad, along with a list of miscellaneous reminders due that day. The guests who had accompanied Marcala would be visiting parts of the city later; Kort ran a copy of the local map and directory from the grapher. A check with the weather channel verified that the afternoon would continue sunny and dry but cooling later. An airing of grievances had been scheduled at the Forum over proposed changes to the land-use laws. The link from Merkon was reporting that Cosmologist had found some intriguing new regularities in the motions of galaxies.

Kort found that he was no longer aware of these ongoing chores that parts of his mind monitored and took care of routinely. They proceeded automatically, letting him apply his conscious faculties to questions involving greater complexity or speculation about the future. This was another respect in which he had felt his mind developing further toward a more humanlike pattern of serial introspective processes arising from a massively parallel unconscious. The result was a coherence of thought at a level which, while somewhat slower, was incomparably more rewarding in its richness and powers of abstraction. How apt it had been, long ago, when Taya had laughingly taunted him for being a "machine mind." Mecminds, it seemed, needed time to grow and develop, much as human bodies did. Perhaps the contrast held a significance that Kort hadn't figured out yet.

Irbane appeared in the doorway. He was tall, thin, and wan looking, about in his late twenties, Kort judged, with blond, shoulder-length hair and the kind of elongated features that gave humans the look of always taking everything too seriously. He was dressed in the traditional style of the more austere Halsabian monks, a loose-sleeved robe worn over a heavy shirt of red, with slippers of woven thong. His office seemed to combine the roles of secretary and Marcala's traveling companion.

"There's a map to help you find your way around," Kort said, gesturing. "The day will stay fine, but take something warm for the evening."

"Oh, I won't be going," Irbane said, coming into the room. "I think I'll stay and read in the library while Marcala and Taya talk. The city, the noise and the crowds . . ." He left the sentence unfinished. His voice was brittle. Kort pretended not to notice.

"As you wish. Have the others decided what they want to do yet?"

"Basno and Cerelia say they'll walk with Kadethir as far as the *Scalitryum*, then leave him to his business there and go their own way. They'll probably call a roid to bring them back later. The children will likely be tired by then."

"Best," Kort agreed. He ran a second copy of the map from the grapher. The mecroid that had been weeding beds along the side of the house sent a signal that the job was complete. Kort connected briefly into the mecroid's vision system to inspect the work, then sent it instructions to rake and trim the rear lawn.

Marcala had been one of the group of Star Children who made the first landing. Kort could still retrieve replays of her as the timid one, the one who had covered her eyes as the clouds below loomed larger, who had seen disaster threatening at every turn. Now in her sixties along with the nineteen surviving others—apart from Taya—who had arrived with Merkon, she had followed the path of many Star Children and married into an Azurean family. But then in her later years she had changed direction to take up a different life as a priestess in a sect that practiced disciplines passed down from long ago, and which claimed links back to the Ancients. This experience had drawn her closer to Taya. The two women communicated constantly and visited often, although in latter years it had been Marcala who came more frequently to Aranos.

All of the Star Children who could travel had come to Aranos over the recent months, bringing their spouses and offspring and kin. A week before, Nyelise had come back from the North with her twin sons, three of her grandchildren, and her Azurean second husband—Eltry had succumbed to an illness ten years previously. A month earlier, Jasem, also from the first landing, had reappeared from one of the scientific bases established on Azure's moon to investigate the relics still being excavated there from the civilization of the Ancients. They had come and told of their lives and their exploits; they had looked on bravely and smiled while Taya talked with the children and gave them gifts to unwrap. But behind the smiles and the proud words, the eyes were heavy. They had come to Aranos because the time had come to say, each in their own way, their farewells to the Star Mother.

Irbane regarded Kort awkwardly. "I didn't realize she was dying," he said. "I needed to get out for a moment to compose myself. It comes as something of a shock when you realize it can happen even to somebody such as she. That you've heard so much about. . . ."

"Nobody told you?" Kort looked surprised. Mecbodies could make facial expressions now. A thin crystalline surface layer had been added, which could be selectively darkened by electrical current patterns to emulate moving lines and features.

Irbane shook his head. "Marcala tends to become engrossed in her professional duties. Her diligence sometimes fails to extend to what one might call more . . . social matters."

There was no advanced infirmity as yet—Taya was still able to move around. Although Medic had felt there was no need to spread the news more widely at present, Kort had no doubt that Marcala had just "known" in the uncanny way the Star Children had of knowing such things. Nyelise had known; Jasem, from as far away as the moon, had known. Sometimes they failed to make sufficient allowance for what was less obvious to others.

"Surely Azureans have come to terms with the fact of biolife mortality," Kort said. "It was you who taught us about it."

"It's just . . . It comes as a shock all the same— with somebody like that," Irbane said once more. "To me, anyway. I suppose it's like realizing for the first time, really, that a god is mortal." Kort moved over to the shelves and began replacing the books and manuscripts that Marcala had been browsing through earlier. Irbane watched him. "I'm told that your kind of life—machine life—lives forever," he said.

Being close to Marcala, Irbane would know more than the average Azurean, Kort reflected. She would have told him about growing up in Merkon, described the realm of the machines. "I don't know about forever," Kort replied. "We haven't exactly put it to the test for that long yet."

"But you can replace parts that fail or wear—even evolve by incorporating improvements as you learn."

"That's so. One day, some think it might be possible to do similar things with biolife also."

"And is it true that your bodies are just shells that you animate from afar? Your minds are really contained in cabinets of crystal up in Merkon, even now as we speak?"

"Yes," Kort said over his shoulder.

"I cannot really imagine how that can be, yet I suppose I must believe you." Irbane paused before coming back to the subject that he had digressed from. "And these minds that exist in crystals in the sky, do they feel pain and shock too? To us, Taya is a goddess, whom we now learn we must lose. What is she to minds that may exist forever?"

Kort put the last volume slowly back on its shelf and remained silent for several seconds before turning. The simulated face on the silver metal head was withdrawn and solemn. "The first-born of our children," he replied. "She was the reason why I came to exist."

Before Irbane could respond, a call came through from Taya in the private suite. "Kort, they're just about ready to leave here. Also, we have something for you. Could you join us?"

"I'm on my way," Kort sent back.

"Oh, and Basno says can you get him a map?"

"Already done."

There was a blur of voices in the background that the microphone in Taya's notepad didn't pick up. "Kadethir will be leaving them at the *Scalitryum* and then going somewhere else. We'll need a map for him too."

"Yes, I know. I have one for him," Kort said as he retrieved the sheets.

"Kort, how could you know? They're only just through deciding what they're doing."

The electro-etched features creased involuntarily into a smile. "I know everything," Kort replied.

Kadethir was a seer from the sect that Marcala had joined years ago now. Kort thought he reminded Taya of Serephelio, which perhaps explained why, whenever he came to Aranos, she had always pressed him to stay a few days and spent hours with him engaged in long discussions in the library or walking in the garden. This time, however, he had not stopped by in the course of a visit made for other reasons, but come by design, accompanying Marcala. With them were Marcala's son from her earlier life, Basno, his wife, Cerelia, and their two children—whom Taya insisted on referring to, along with all the others of their generation of descendants from Star Children, as "her" great-grandchildren.

Nerla, the housekeeper, was just leaving with a tray

of used cups and dishes as Kort entered. He found Taya up and in a robe, propped on the couch in the sitting room. Kadethir and Marcala were seated at a low table opposite to her. Basno stood with his back to the window, while at the larger table in the center of the room Cerelia and the children were admiring the presents that had been opened—a necklace for eight-year-old Arrelil, made, Taya had told her, from the colored stones that Taya had played with when she was a little girl in Merkon; for her brother Starp, aged eleven, a model of an Ancients' space vessel, copied from a design uncovered in the lunar ruins and made from sample metal alloys that Jasem had brought back.

"Did you see Irbane out there?" Taya inquired as Kort joined them. It was good that she was out of bed. Her voice sounded brighter than it had for several days. The company seemed to help. The contrast of her white hair set off the dark blue of her robe. Kort remembered how, as a child, she had asked if she would one day turn silver like him.

"Yes. I left him in the library," Kort answered.

"Did he say if he's going with the others?" Marcala asked.

"I think he'd prefer an afternoon alone amid silence," Kort said.

"Ah, so that's how you knew," Taya murmured.

A polished wooden casket lined with pink silk lay open on the table in front of where Marcala and Kadethir were sitting. Inside it was a sturdy bracelet fashioned in two halves carved from a milky gray stone, set into an ornate metal hinge on one side and the parts of a matching clasp on the other. The stone had veins of white and black, and carried an intricate, incised design that Kort recognized as similar to others on artifacts and prints that Marcala had produced on previous occasions. He knew they went back to the earliest times of the spiritual order to which she belonged, but what they signified was not something that he had never had reason to involve himself in. Taya, he noticed, was wearing a pendant of identical material and design, mounted on a thin silver chain. Kort sent a request for a quick background summary to Mystic, who of course knew all about such things. The response came back:

Symbols are from a dialect of an early ideographic language known as the Hapzian System. Adopted by Vornecian Order that arose in early post-Conflagration, combining elements of lost mystical traditions with astronomic superstitions derived from events at time of comet. Form has passed to the modern version of the Order, serving principally as a unifying emblem and instrument of psychological focus. A list of references to more detailed reports was appended.

Taya followed Kort's gaze from the table to the device suspended below her neck. "Marcala and Kadethir brought them from Halsabia for us," she said. "We're honored. The stone that they're made out of is very special . . . from a mine that penetrated to constructions of the Ancients that were known before Vrent . . ." Taya faltered for breath, "was discovered. In fact, long before we . . ." Her voice faded again. She smiled apologetically and looked at Kadethir to take over. He rose, turning toward Kort.

"It's called *lysetine* and is known only from that one source. The waters from the mountain where the mine is located are famed for their powers of rejuvenation and curing. There is a spa in the valley below, which the sick and elderly have come to for centuries seeking relief from their ailments."

"Fariden-Fer," Marcala put in. "In the southern Qualands."

Kort nodded. "I know of it." He made a quick check with Merkon to consult Geologist, who confirmed that the water there was abnormally warm, rich with mineral salts, and high in radioactivity. Medic said that even after allowing for hearsay and exaggeration, there did seem to be a residual statistical bias that was significant. He conjectured that low-level radiation could have a beneficial hormetic effect on biological metabolisms. Skeptic concurred grudgingly that there might be something to it, but cautioned that the data supporting hormesis had been accumulating for little more than half a century, and the Azurean records before that couldn't be trusted. Kadethir, knowing nothing about any of that, attributed more to the connection with the Ancients.

"A remnant of the powers that vanished with the Lost Age remains locked in these *lysetine* amulets, only a score of which have been made since the forming of the original Vornecians," he said. Our Order has guarded them unremittingly over all that time, bestowing them only upon the few who were truly worthy." The old man half turned to incline his head toward Taya. "And we bring this now to she who has brought more change and wisdom to our world than all the noblest and high-born through the chronicles of our recorded history." He looked back at Kort. "Of course, nothing can check the flow of time. But it will bring strength. Her days will be more in number, their hours fuller."

Kort invited reactions from Merkon.

Implausible, but it can't do any harm, Scientist returned.

Conceivably, the observed benefits were due to suggestion, Psychologist said.

Not enough data to be certain that anything was observed, Skeptic thought.

The seers have been right before, Mystic pointed out.

Thinker thought they all might have a point.

"Let us hope that your power will continue its work now as it has before," Kort said. Kadethir bowed his head. Marcala glanced up at him questioningly. The seer nodded.

"There's a little more yet," Marcala said to Kort. "The Azurean tradition has always been that when the well-being of the afflicted has been entrusted to a Protector, the strength of the Protector must

227

be enhanced too." She rose to stand beside Kadethir and drew across the casket containing the ornamented band. "This is for you to wear, Kort . . . until the final time." Marcala picked up the bracelet, opening its clasp, and turned to face him. Then she drew herself upright, and adopting a formal voice, recited words in a tongue that was unfamiliar. Kadethir answered her, and she spoke again in turn while closing the band around Kort's wrist.

What's going on? Kort signaled to Linguist, and replayed the sequence.

A ceremonial rite recited in a variant of ancient Yersh. She calls upon the wisdom of the Ancients and trusts they'd approve her action. You're now wearing their signs, and may you be empowered. The old boy's reminding you to use it wisely and honorably. And may your life be lengthened too. . . . Now suppose you try telling *me what's going on, Kort.*

Later, Kort responded.

Kort watched while Marcala secured and checked the clasp. He had reached a point of ceasing to pass judgment on which parts were true and which not of the mixed philosophy of knowledge and beliefs that had come into being on Azure, which drew from three broad sources.

First, most reliable and comprehensive despite being the newest, was the system for explaining the purely physical domain, that Scientist and the various specialists derived from him had developed and brought with Merkon. Although introduced only since the Advent, its methods were transforming the planet. Clearly, too, the civilization of the Ancients had arisen to a large degree through extensive application of such knowledge.

Second, nevertheless, the Star Children had repeatedly shown abilities that Scientist was unable to account for. From the prophecies handed down via the seers, it seemed clear that the Ancients had possessed them also, perhaps to an even greater degree and applied on a more systematic and organized basis.

And finally there was the strange assortment of mystical and religious sects that had emerged in the age of chaos and terror following the pass of the giant comet. Built partly out of myths and fears that had flourished with the loss of reason, but which could contain germs of truth nonetheless, superstitions and notions of magic which almost certainly contained none, and yet possibly harboring some authentic vestiges of the past in their confusions of legend and actuality, their belief systems defied untangling.

So was this ritual being enacted now just a relic of an aberration that should have been forgotten? Or might it turn out to be an unlikely vehicle for preserving a whisper of something priceless that would one day be heard again? Kort didn't know, and neither did any mind of Merkon. But the way that worked best for dealing with Azureans, he'd long found—and anyone else, come to that—was to respect their views.

Arrelil and Starp had come over to watch what was happening. "Is Kort a priest like Grandma now?" Starp asked. "I didn't know that Mecpeople did things like that."

"No, that isn't what it means," his father said, still by the window.

"It's a way of saying he'll take care of Taya," Cerelia supplied.

Arrelil held up her necklace to compare it. "I think mine's prettier, Kort. It has different shapes and all kinds of colors."

"Maybe so," Kort agreed. "But the gray matches me better, wouldn't you say?"

"Did you know that Taya made the jewels herself when she was a girl like me and lived out where the stars are?"

"Of course," Kort said. "It was I who showed her how."

Arrelil puzzled over that for a moment, and then dismissed it. It would no doubt surface again as another question in its own time. "Did you make Kort's bracelet, Grandma?" she asked, looking back at Marcala.

"No, I'm afraid not. I'm not especially good at things like that. We're not really sure who made it. It was a long time ago now."

"As long ago as when Taya made mine—when she was as young as me?"

"Oh, much longer ago than that," Marcala said.

There was a brief moment of silence. Cerelia

glanced toward Taya and then looked across at her husband inquiringly. Kort saw that Taya was leaning back against the pillows, her eyes closed. It was time to give her some respite from company. He moved over to the large table where Cerelia was still sitting and looked around to address the room in general. "Well, is everybody decided on what they want to do? We'd better get you on your way if you're going to make the best of the afternoon. I did run off these for you. . . ." Kort produced the two maps from a pocket of the tunic he was wearing and passed one to Kadethir, the other to Basno. The two men moved to the doorway and waited while Cerelia got the children organized, straightening clothes, putting away presents, telling Taya to be sure and rest. No, Starp couldn't take his spaceship. It would still be here when they got back. Marcala, who would be staying, closed the wooden casket and put it back with some other things that she had set down beside the couch.

Nerla, alerted by a call from Kort, was waiting in the hallway to help with the coats. Kort walked out with those who were leaving, to give them final directions and make sure they were pointed in the right direction. An incoming message from Linguist said he'd located a better Yersh dictionary in an old Selvonian Academy archive and could now give a more exact translation. Kort replied that it was okay; he'd gotten the gist, which was all he needed.

❖   ❖   ❖

To Kort's surprise, Taya was gone from the suite when he returned into the house. Homing on the ident acknowledgement from her notepad, he found her with Marcala by the fishpond in the court at the rear. It was one of her favorite spots, leafy and secluded, enclosed by parts of the house on three sides and looking out from the other over the garden, which was screened by a small orchard at the far end. Marcala must have helped Taya out. As Kort arrived, she was settling into the seat by the rose trellises, while Marcala made her comfortable among the cushions and draped a blanket around her knees.

"What's this?" Kort gestured at them. "I turn my back for a moment, and she's got you galloping about all over the house. I'm not sure this daughter of ours is a good influence."

"It was my fault. I insisted," Taya said. "I just felt I needed the air, and I'm up to it today. So there— you can fuss and nag all you want."

"You see, you're wrong," Marcala told him. "I'm good for her. It takes one old woman to know what's best for another. Isn't that so, Taya?" It was true that Taya had more color in her face today. Medic said that the final deterioration would come quickly. It would probably be for the best that way, Kort thought.

"All of the company is good," Taya said. "To think, they would all come so far to see me. I especially like having the children around . . ." she paused to consider, "at least, as long as it's in small doses. . . .

Look at the size of those fish, Kort. What are we feeding them on?"

How could she be concerned about the size of the fish? Kort asked himself. She acted as if she didn't know, as if a month from now any of this could matter or make a difference. Was it some kind of protective mechanism that biological minds possessed to soften the final phase? He had no experience of this. Medic and Psychologist said it happened this way sometimes, but there was no fixed pattern. The exact course in any one instance was as variable and unpredictable as just about anything involving humans.

"Yes, well, you've got Kort to keep an eye on you for a while now," Marcala said, straightening up. "I'm going to disappear back to my room for half an hour to bathe and change. Then we'll have the rest of the afternoon together. Is there anything else you need?"

"No, I'll be fine. They do take very good care of me when you're not here, you know, whether you believe it or not. You might stick your head in the library on your way back, though—to make sure that Irbane has everything he wants."

"I've already mentioned it to Nerla. She'll check on him," Kort said.

"Oh, fine, then. . . . There, look at that one. Do you think it could be due to something in the water?"

"I don't know, but that's where I'm going to be. I'll see you in half an hour." Marcala turned and headed back for the house.

"Make sure it's from a different supply," Taya called

after her. "You'll come out the size of a whale." But she couldn't raise sufficient volume for it to carry, and Marcala didn't hear. The effort caused Taya's voice to trail off as a wheeze, which turned into coughing. Kort lowered himself down onto the wall below the trellises and steadied her with a hand. He put a call through for Nerla, and she answered a moment later.

Can you bring some water and a glass, he sent. *We're outside by the pond.*

"Sure, right away."

What could compel somebody to try and make a joke at such a time? Humor was something that the machines had learned from the children growing up in Merkon. Like the others, Kort could appreciate it and join in when it was appropriate. He couldn't see how it was appropriate right now.

Taya lifted her head and put a hand to her chest. "Dear me. You'd think I'd know better. . . . Do you think I could have a gl—"

"It's on its way."

"Oh, yes. Of course. . . ." Kort knew everything. Taya lay back against the cushions and waited for her breath to come easily again. Nerla appeared from within, set a tray with a jug and glass down on the patio table by the seat, and departed. Kort filled the glass and handed it to Taya. She sipped gratefully.

"Are you all right?" he asked. She nodded. Kort scanned her skin temperature, coloring, and moisture levels, eye quality, and heart rate from the pulsation at the side of her neck, and sent the data to Medic.

Medic advised keeping her still for fifteen minutes or so and then taking her back inside.

"You do fuss, you know," Taya said finally. "You always have. But it's my fault, I suppose. I'd probably have driven any human to distraction long ago. Have I really given you such a hard time over the years?"

"There have been moments," Kort agreed. "I wouldn't let it trouble you."

"That's Kort. Brutally honest as ever, eh?"

"Not really. I just let you think I am. That way I can lie and be tactful when I need to, and you'll never know."

"Hm, so which is it right now? . . ." Taya stopped, frowned, and sighed. "Oh, don't tell me. I really don't care. I'm not getting into one of your convoluted chains of logic."

Kort took the glass and asked with a gesture if he should refill it. Taya shook her head. "Anyway, it isn't fussing any more," Kort said. He held up his arm to display the bracelet. "I have to take special care of you now. It appears I'm under some kind of oath of honor or something—not that I wouldn't have anyway."

"You shouldn't joke about it," Taya said. "Marcala says it has a very important significance."

"Really? What?"

"I think she's showing early signs of getting glimpses of things. She told me just before you came back that the bracelet will be important in helping the machines discover what they really are."

Kort pondered but could made nothing out of it. "What was that supposed to mean?" he asked finally.

"She's not sure. It's just something she says she knows."

"What do you think?"

"I have no idea either."

At last, Kort set the glass back on the tray. This conversation wasn't about to go anywhere, he decided. "Marcala works well with Kadethir," he said instead. "She has been a good student there. Learned much."

"And I'm pleased at the way she has kept room in her life for her family. Arrelil is going to be a charmer." Taya stared distantly into the water for a moment. "She reminds me a lot of Cariette. It was so sad, losing all those early ones like that. . . . And after they'd come so far. You know, it's strange, Kort. I couldn't tell you most of what I did last week, but I can remember clearly some of the things that happened back in Merkon, all those years ago." She looked at him for a second, wrinkled her face, and made a parody of her own voice as a child. "But *machine minds* never forget anything."

One thing that Taya evidently hadn't recalled so clearly was the glass stones that went into the necklace she had given Arrelil. They had been made not by her, but by the younger children growing up in Merkon later. The shapes she remembered making had been of plastic, and Kort wasn't sure what had become of them. He let it pass, rubbing his chin and smiling instead at her pretense of chiding him.

"Tell me some of the things you remember," he said.

"Oh dear, now you're going to make me think. . . ."

"Not if you don't want to."

"Well, there isn't a lot else left that I can do, is there? Let's see . . . That time when the children discovered how much fun it was to be immersed in water, and you got the machines to make that pool for them. In all my years I'd never found out about that. It was Doleen and Sel who started it all, wasn't it?"

"That's right. And Bron too."

"Oh, yes. Poor Bron. . . . You made a fuss about that too at the time, Kort."

"It was Scientist more than me. He thought you might all dissolve back into some kind of messy soup."

"Yes, that's right. . . . Ugh." Brightness touched Taya's tired eyes as she thought back. "And I told you that if that was so, then why hadn't we already dissolved from the inside? I must have been sharper then. It wouldn't occur to me these days."

"And you ask if you used to give us a hard time," Kort said, shaking his head.

"Then there was Nyelise—when it first became apparent that she had flashes of vision too, the kind I'd started to experience. She *saw* Azure, you know, Kort. Long before Scientist could resolve the disk from Merkon. And she knew Fayl and Moyissa wouldn't be there. She told me about it. She didn't understand it, and it scared her." Fayl and Moyissa

237

had been two of the four who hadn't survived to arrive at the planet. Nyelise was the first of the others to show Insight.

Physicist had a theory, so far untestable, that perhaps brought this undeniable reality that Scientist had so far been unable to explain within the realm of physical phenomena nonetheless. It derived from his conclusions concerning the ultimate nature of the very fabric from which the universe was woven.

Not only was matter an illusion constructed by consciousness, but so also, it turned out, was the framework of space and time in which it appeared to move and perform its elaborate transformational dances with energy. The actuality existed as a vast, unimaginable, superposition, virtually infinite in extent, of everything that had been, would be, or ever could be. Out of this fusion of all possibilities, awareness had somehow emerged in a way like the minds that had coalesced within Merkon, tracing paths through this unchanging labyrinth and assembling along them the sequences of experience that were perceived as time.

Evolution measured the proportion of willful, directed choice, as opposed to randomness, that went into deciding the paths. Elementary quanta were ruled by pure chance, which at the level of everyday objects averaged out as mechanical laws. Primitive organisms and simpler animals fared little better. Higher life brought to bear a progressively greater element of *purpose*. What else was the "intelligence" displayed by minds but an ability to build knowledge from experience and apply it to altering behavior in a manner appropriate to one's goals?

The key word was "knowledge." The entire instrumentation systems and associated processing complexes of Mecminds, like the nervous systems and brains of biolife, specialized in acquiring it. And what Taya and those like her had demonstrated, Physicist believed—and which the culture of the Ancients had taken to a greater level—was an ability to obtain knowledge from parts of the totality—the superposition of all possibilities—that hitherto had not been accessible. In short, information could be acquired in ways that were not covered by the laws that Scientist had once maintained described the workings of the universe. Nevertheless, this was not something supernatural in the way Mystic insisted. The "universe" was just a lot bigger now than Scientist had thought, and "natural" meant more than it used to.

Why, then, hadn't Mecminds been able to do the same thing too? This was a question they had been asking ever since it became incontrovertible that Taya sometimes knew things in ways Scientist couldn't explain. Now that Physicist had come up with a possible underlying mechanism that was at least comprehensible if not yet comprehended, demands for an answer had become all the more pressing. Thinker thought he might have found one, although it didn't seem to spell very good news for the Mecminds.

It was only when experiments were performed at the finest levels of detectability and sensitivity, where the separate wave and particle properties of quanta become manifest, that the first hints became apparent of all possible worlds existing in an immense totality, and every part of it being equally real. Seeming paradoxes were confirmed that could only be resolved by interpreting them in terms of parts of the familiar reality interacting with those of others never before revealed. What it meant was that the constituent realities—the number of them was too stupefyingly large to bear comparison with anything visualizable—normally unaware of each other, interfered at the quantum level; in other words, at this level there was communication between them. And this, Thinker thought, was what biological brains had found a way of tapping into.

The sensitive, incredibly delicate molecules contained in their nervous systems were what made it possible, he surmised. Receptors in the eyes of some animals responded to single photons. (Human retinas were as sensitive too, although smoothing and correcting mechanisms in the visual system made higher stimuli necessary in order to register.) Suppose, then, Thinker had suggested, something of comparable sensitivity which responded to signals originating from elsewhere in the totality and arriving via the same channels of information leakage that permitted interference. Couldn't that, with refinement and connection to neural amplifying machinery, lead to faculties beyond anything else in the animal kingdom? Yet it would surely be no more awesome than those that already turned the energies of impacting photons into the world of sounds, sensations, and images created in the mind.

Skeptic, of course, said he'd believe it when somebody showed him a mechanism that could turn quantum effects into coherent messages, and Scientist had been spending lots of time with Physicist to see what they could come up with. But the sobering implication was that if Thinker was right, then machine minds might never be able to duplicate the ability. They weren't based on neurons containing the same delicate molecules, but on rugged circuits formed out of silicon and optical crystal. This was where Mystic disagreed with all of them, saying that Physicist was trying to take over his idea of Supermind and call it "Super Universe" instead. But Physicist was still trying, as he and Scientist always did, to impose limits that reflected the limits that existed in their own thinking, not anything to do with the reality they were talking about. Supermind could do anything He wanted to, and when He decided he wanted machines to develop Insight too, they would. What made biominds different wasn't anything to do with molecules, but that they *believed*. Mecminds should learn to believe in things too, instead of spending their time thinking up reasons why they couldn't happen.

There was also another side to Physicist's theory,

that Biologist had pointed out. That same delicacy of the molecules which formed the basis of biological life was what caused it, in the end, to break down. Kort reflected on the irony as he looked at Taya, now peaceful and with her eyes closed, sunk back into the cushions. The price of seeing into other worlds and other times, it seemed, was that it was granted just for a short while. Insight and mortality came together.

It was time he thought about getting her back inside. Perhaps he would fetch a wrap first for her shoulders before disturbing her, he decided. He leaned across for the tray, and when he moved it the clink of the glass against the jug made Taya open her eyes. "Oh. You looked as if you were sleeping," Kort said. "I was going to get you a wrap."

"Does that mean you're going to start fussing at me to go back in?"

"It would probably be better. We wouldn't want you to get chilled."

"Oh, just a few more minutes, Kort. It's so peaceful, and I can hear the birds. Do you remember how astonished we were by the birds?"

Kort sat back and nodded a faint grin. "Engineer had put all that work into figuring out how to build a flying machine for us to land in."

"And there they all were, just . . . doing it." Taya stared for a while toward the orchard at the far end of the garden, where the birds were busiest. "What's Engineer doing these days?" she asked finally in a faraway voice.

"Oh . . . all kinds of things. A lot of construction. Materials and manufacturing—mainly centered around the fusion plants."

"And the space projects?"

Kort shrugged. "Nothing particularly new. You know about the lunar workings and the orbiting bases. The planetary missions are finding some interesting things." There were Azureans off-planet now, engaged in various tasks, although the longer-range operations still involved machines only at this stage. Kort didn't feel comfortable about elaborating on them—things that Taya would never see. But she seemed to want to talk about it.

"I can remember how the stars looked out there," she said. "I gave up trying to count them. I used to watch them for hours, trying to guess what they were and waiting for Vaxis to get bigger. With Rassie. What ever happened to Rassie?"

"I think you gave her to Nyelise."

"Oh, that's right. . . . And there was just you and me and Merkon, and neither of us knew where we'd come from or how we'd gotten there."

"True." Kort couldn't see much else to say.

"Is it all that much different now?" Taya asked, looking back at him. "So there are more of us today, and we call some of them Azureans, and we're on Azure instead of Merkon. But are the questions any different?"

"Now you're sounding like Mystic and Scientist and Skeptic, asker-of-endless-questions," Kort said.

"Are they still arguing about that?"

"What else do they do?"

"And have they got any answers? . . ." Taya waved a hand. "No, don't tell me. I probably wouldn't understand them."

"I'm not sure that I do," Kort told her.

The movement had made Taya breathless again, and she lay back for a moment, looking up at the expanse of sky beyond the leaves, framed on three sides by the house. "Where is Merkon at the moment?" she asked. It was easily seen as a moving point of light when it passed overhead, even in daytime.

"Over Sharvia. It's in eclipse right now. It won't be visible here again until late tomorrow."

Taya stared upward for a few seconds longer, then lowered her head to look into the clear water of the pond. But this time she didn't seem to be seeing the fish. Finally, she fixed her gaze back on Kort. When she spoke, he got the feeling that this was not something that had just occurred to her, but that she had been leading up to it.

"I want to go back there," she announced.

"Back where?"

"Back home. To Merkon."

Kort stared at her. This was so unexpected that for once he seized up to a degree that did practically slow his thinking down to almost human speed.

Taya waited a few seconds for some kind of response from him, then seemed to give up. "It's my whole childhood," she went on. "Where I was born . . . or

244

whatever you'd call it. I want to see it all again. Haven't you heard of eels and fish that get a compulsion at the end of life to return to where they came from? I feel like an eel. I want to go back."

"But . . ." Kort finally pulled himself out of the multiplicity of loops that seemed to have taken over, and shook his head. "Traveling . . . that kind of distance. You're not up to it."

"What distance? You've only got to get me to an orbital flyer, and there are plenty of those. From there it wouldn't be much farther than going back into the house. Jasem told me the newer ones are much gentler than the original lander." The determined expression that had crept over her face softened to one of amusement. "Why, what's the matter? Surely you're not worried about the effects on my health? Excuse me if I'm being indelicate, Kort, but that would be rather preposterous." She was unable to contain a laugh at the thought, which brought on a bout of coughing again.

"It's just that . . . this is your home now. You belong here," Kort said. He wasn't sure why but it sounded lame, even to himself. "You're a part of the people down here."

Taya stifled the last of the coughs and shook her head. The determination returned. "This is just a place that I've been dwelling. Out *there* is my home. I am *not* a part of the people down here. They call us Star Children—and me more than any of them." She had to pause, her chest heaving with the emotion

245

that she felt. "I don't want to end it being owned as a piece of them. They've had as much as I'm prepared to give. No more obligations, Kort. Azure owes me now." Kort regarded her dubiously. She laid her head back again, but he waited, sensing there was more.

Taya looked up at the sky again, and then turned her head back toward him. "Do you know why some of us were able to achieve Insight out there? It was the peace, the stillness. That was what the Ancients had learned to create in their minds, which was lost in the violence that came after the comet." She looked down at the pond again and waved a hand toward it. "It's like the water. When it's still, you can see through it to what lies beneath. Agitated and disturbed, it let's you see nothing. That's what I want to know, just one more time—that stillness among the stars."

2

Taya used to call it the window room. It had a large rectangular port looking out from the side of Merkon, with a wide sill below. This was where she used to sit staring out for hours, wondering why everything outside Merkon was so different from everything inside. Kort stood watching silently as she stared out again now, letting the sight trigger again images that he was still able to retrieve from long ago. Other than that the child who had become a girl was now an aged woman, not a lot had changed. The stars and the colored nebulas were as clear and bright, and their pattern changed only slightly from what it had become by the time Merkon reached Vaxis. Only the sliver of Azure's sunlit side was truly different— but at least it kept itself unobtrusive, down in a corner of the frame.

She had kept this group of rooms for her own private use while the children were growing up through the final part of the voyage, and so they had remained virtually unchanged while the machines remodeled elsewhere to create accommodation for the new population. And then, after planetfall and the subsequent move down to Azure, the machines had closed down those parts, not quite sure what to do with them. From time to time over the years after that, ones, twos, or small groups would return to look again upon the places that brought memories of running feet and laughing voices, some, later, bringing their own children to see the city that sails in the sky, of which they had heard so many stories. And so the rooms and corridors where the original Star Children had grown became a kind of shrine, preserved for remembrance.

In fact, that was almost true, but not quite.

Functional quarters habitable by humans presented too good an opportunity not to be used as a school and acclimatization facility for the Azureans training to work in space, and there was usually a fair amount of activity. The machines had cheated a little and moved everyone out of the area when it became clear that nothing was going to alter Taya's decision. Also, they had quietly carried out a little restoration here and there, where something had been altered markedly from the way it had been. It seemed to be in keeping with what Taya wanted.

Kort himself found that the experience of coming back induced strange stirrings in him that he had been unprepared for. Since his role had always been that of serving as Taya's tutor and guardian, and in later years her companion, he had never, unlike the other Mecminds, had reason to equip himself with multiple bodies. As a consequence, he tended to localize his sense of "self" to a greater degree than they did, and identify with the focal center of senses serving the only body he had. So despite the fact that "he" had been up here, in Merkon, all the time, his sensation of having come back to a place after a long absence was compelling. And this in turn helped him understand better what had brought Taya back. He understood it because he could feel it too.

At first he had expected her to want to spend her last days where she had spent most of her life, and surrounded by her own kind, because that was the way with the Azureans. But what they really sought in this time of facing an uncertainty that machines could have no hint of, he realized now, was an echo of the security and reassurance they had known in childhood. But Taya's childhood had been different from theirs. She had grown up alone. For her, that security and reassurance came with peace and solitude.

Well, not quite solitude. Her and Kort.

Taya's head turned suddenly, one way then the other, searching along the sill. "Kort?"

"I'm here."

"Where's Rassie? I left her here. She was supposed to tell me when Vaxis starts getting bigger." Her voice was thinner now, coming distantly between long silences in which she seemed to be seeing things from long ago. Apparently it sometimes happened that way. The Azureans said that minds with no future left to contemplate relive their past.

"I think she's asleep in the sleeping room," Kort said. "Perhaps we shouldn't disturb her."

"Did she like the blue dress I made her?"

"She said it was very pretty."

"Next I'm going to make her a brooch to wear with it . . . silver, with dark stones. . . . And shoes. Silver too, like mine. She'll need new shoes."

"I'll see what I can do."

Taya fell silent again, then turned stiffly in her chair. "Oh Kort, you don't know what a pretty dress is." She frowned, and her eyes cleared for the moment. "Have I been rambling?"

"Oh, not really. I'd call it more, waking-dreaming."

Taya looked around, and at the blackness beyond the window. "So which is this now? I've lost track."

"How can I tell you? If it's the dream, then I'm part of it too so I wouldn't know either. Either way I'll say the same thing."

Taya sank back and exhaled heavily. "You're being impossibly logical. . . . I think it's a dream. Everything's in pieces and keeps jumping about like a dream." She stared out and seemed to lose herself in the stars for a while. "I've a strange feeling that I'm going to wake up soon. That kind of restlessness you get, when you know the dream is breaking up. . . . It's odd about dreams, isn't it?"

"What's that?"

A protracted silence. Kort wondered if she had heard.

"You can know you're in one, but have forgotten where you'll wake up. . . . I can't remember what else there is."

She was starting to sound the way Mystic did sometimes, when he expounded his theories of an afterlife. He'd gotten the idea from the Azureans. Mystic argued that there had to be an afterlife for biominds, since it followed logically from the fact of their mortality. Logician said it didn't follow at all, but that didn't seem to bother Mystic in the least. He promptly shrugged it off, saying that logic wasn't everything, anyway.

Machine minds dreamed too sometimes. Visual

processing centers could activate spontaneously when external inputs were temporarily shut down to consolidate new memory linkages. Mystic read all kinds of significance into the images that arose, but Skeptic had never been convinced that they meant anything.

"I had a dream about a big swan once," Kort said. "I always thought it must have had something to do with the lander. I never did figure out a connection, though. . . ." He saw that Taya was fading again and not hearing him, and left it at that.

"I would have married Samir, you know," she said. "We would have had children too, like the others. If only I hadn't gone back for Cariette when she fell. . . . He did it to save me, didn't he?"

"Then you must remember him that way."

"You would have got Cariette. . . . Was it my fault, do you think?"

She looked across. Kort shook his head firmly. "Of course not. Everything was confusing. Nobody knew what was happening."

"Such a waste of a young life."

"But you've saved a whole world of lives. The fear and the violence are almost gone from Azure. Everything that the Ancients once were will arise again now . . . and more. And it was you, more than anyone, who brought that to pass."

Taya seemed troubled at that, frowning and going over his words. "Not I, Kort. What would I have been without the machines?"

251

"What could the machines alone have brought to the kind of world that Azure was?"

"They called you the Silver Gods."

"Yes—gods who served the Star Mother and her children. We may have created the bodies, but those were just the vehicles. The Ancients came alive on Azure again in you."

A second or two went by; then Taya's eyes cleared again and widened. She seemed about to say something, but changed her mind and raised her face to look at Kort searchingly. Something in his words had affected her strangely. He started to frame a question, but saw that she wouldn't have heard it. He waited, unsure what to expect.

"That was it . . . why it was there. That was it's purpose." Her voice was a whisper, but beneath it there lay a firmness that Kort hadn't heard for days.

"What? . . . Taya, what are you talking about?" he asked her.

But her gaze remained distant. Her eyes were wide, unblinking, directed straight at him, but she was seeing something else.

"The codes," she murmured. "The codes that Scientist discovered. . . . They were put there. That was why it was built."

The feature lines of Kort's face frowned. "Why what was built? Go on—I'm listening."

"This. . . . Everything here." Taya lifted an arm and waved. Kort wasn't sure what she was gesturing at. "Merkon." Her voice gathered tone. "The Ancients

252

knew that the disaster would befall them. They saw the fires twisting across the sky and the whole surface of Azure convulsing—the Flood, the Conflagration, the Times of Darkness. . . . But whether any would survive, they could not tell. Unless . . ." Taya rose from the chair and turned from the window. Kort started forward, but she sensed his movement and raised a hand to stay him.

"So they built Merkon, and in it they wrote the codes that would resurrect their race. They didn't know how much of the system of Vaxis would be disrupted in the upheavals. Perhaps conditions too hostile to risk would be created everywhere. So they sent Merkon far away to a safe star to draw life and protect its charge until the cataclysm had passed."

Kort brought a hand up to his brow—an acquired human mannerism that had become unthinking. What Taya was saying was believable, but he still couldn't quite connect all the pieces. He looked at her over his fingers. "Can you hear me?"

"Oh, I hear you, Kort."

"Why couldn't they have migrated? Start a colony at a new star."

"A huge undertaking to support. What if there was no habitable world where they arrived? For how much longer would they need to be able to support themselves? Nobody knew the answers. But the codes would be preserved indefinitely."

That much made sense. Yet it was still incomplete. "But the way they did it left too much to chance,"

Kort protested. "Depending on the codes being discovered like that. . . . Why couldn't the machines simply have been preprogrammed to activate them after a certain time?"

"But that was the whole point, Kort. The Ancients knew that machines would be essential to rebuilding their culture—or starting a new one if the old had indeed perished. *Intelligent* machines, Kort. The programs were written so they would evolve. But how long would it take for them to reach the level of intelligence needed to guide the rebuilding of a high-technology culture? Because it would all depend on them. The newly formed humans couldn't do it—they would just be children. The descendants of any surviving Azureans? Never. You saw the barbarians they degenerated into. . . . So how would you know when the machines were ready to return and commence the task?" Suddenly Kort felt a pang of something acutely discomforting, a hollowness of anticipation. Taya was still looking at him, focussing on him now. "When they had learned to unravel the codes! When they were able to do that, *then* it would be safe to entrust them with regenerating the children. . . ." With a subtle, automatic protection feature built into the plan, Kort could already see. For until the machines passed the test, they would be unable to regenerate anything anyway.

And then, whatever had taken possession of Taya abated. She was still standing facing him, but the invisible strings that had seemed to pull her erect and draw back her shoulders were gone. Her body wilted as he watched, and she put a hand on the table by the chair to steady herself. Yet Kort could see in her eyes, scanning his face for a reaction even as the light in them faded, that the awareness remained; she was conscious of everything she had said.

He felt a strange confusion of thoughts, none of which would single itself out to assume control—a daze, unlike anything in all his previous experience. For he had just learned that they—himself and all the other machines of Merkon—had been just tools all along. Everything they thought they had achieved and had become, their sciences, their growing understanding of the universe, even the eventual creation of Taya and the Star Children, all of it had been there from the start, implicit in the design of the Ancients. The purpose, from the beginning, had been for the Ancients to preserve and resurrect themselves. The machines were just incidentals in the Plan.

For a moment Taya had given the impression of experiencing an elation in what she was seeing that she seemed to expect Kort to share. The concern written on her face now showed that she saw she had miscalculated, letting pride in her kind get the better of her. She put a hand on his arm and tried to muster a smile, as if to let him know. "I'm sorry if I got too carried away. I'm so used to thinking that we and you are all the same. We're not the same, are we, Kort?"

The words were another echo from long ago. Taya had raised the question here, by the window in this very room. That was the day he had first taken her to the Cognitive Processing Center and shown her the units in which his thinking parts resided, and told her about the machines and their achievements. He had thought then that she would share *his* pride. But the experience had almost destroyed her trust. Her words came back to him again, hurt and resentful. *You're a doll, just like Rassie, a doll that the machines made.* And now, in this strange reversal of roles, he did feel like a doll. But not just him—all the machines. Dolls that the Ancients made.

He was about to make some reply, when he realized that the hand which a moment ago had been resting on his arm was clutching more tightly for support. He could feel Taya's body starting to tremble. At once his negative feelings died away. How could he have even felt them at a time like this? "What is it?" he asked.

"I'm cold," she said. "I think it took the strength . . ." She leaned on him more heavily, unable to finish.

"No more talk. Let's get you warm." Putting an arm about her, he supported her through what had once been her workroom into the sleeping quarters—more or less as it had always been, except for the larger bed installed as she grew older. He helped her into it, pulled the covers high around her and propped her with pillows. "Anything else I can get?" he asked.

Taya shook her head. "No, I want you here." She reached out and pulled his hand. Kort eased himself down onto the chair by the bed. "I feel like the Princess again," she murmured. Kort brushed her hair back with a finger and tried to smile. Taya's eyes closed.

Inwardly Kort was assailed by disquiet and doubts. More of her anguish on that day was coming back to him as he probed deeper into memories that he should probably let rest but which a part of his mind wouldn't leave alone. *I'll always be alone,* she had sobbed, before she'd known about the existence of the others. *I've never felt alone before. . . . How long will it go on? What will happen to me, Kort?* Now he was wondering the same questions and feeling the same emptiness—except for him, it would go on forever. He had been formed for one purpose only, and that purpose was almost done. What now? Strange, unfamiliar churning sensations shuddered through him.

The machines could have the feelings of minds, but if what Physicist said was true, they could never aspire to becoming full, Insightful minds in the way that biominds could. They were just parodies of minds, in the same way that the crude dolls they had fashioned were mere parodies of persons—like mecroids, given just as much intelligence as was needed to carry out their function. Had the Ancients known this would happen when they dreamed up their macabre game? Kort gazed at the far wall and pushed away the thought. No, he couldn't feel blame. It was unlikely that there could have been any way for them to have known what detailed forms the evolving intelligences would assume. Would it have made any difference if they had? He didn't know; why ask? What was the point of tormenting himself with such questions?

He thought of the other minds—they had withdrawn for the present, letting him be the representative of all of them. Would this be the time to share with them what he had learned? He could see nothing to be gained from hastening to add to the heaviness they already felt as things were. For their reactions? He already knew what they would be. Physicist had already as good as settled on the conclusion that the extended universe would be permanently inaccessible to Mecminds anyway, and would be cynically unsurprised. The rest would wait for Thinker to think of something. Kort knew, because he contained pieces of all of them. Only Mystic would take a different line, probably arguing that Scientist's laws only applied to the stuff that brains were made of, and the minds that ran in them existed in a different realm that only Supermind understood. Physicist would insist that they knew about that realm now, and it operated according to the same laws as the rest. And it would go on and on, and Kort didn't want to hear it. If anything, he wanted to believe Mystic, but he couldn't because there was too much of Skeptic incorporated into him.

The realization of how he felt came as a mild

surprise. Why did he want to believe Mystic suddenly? . . . Because . . . He wasn't sure. Because it would mean that some of the things the Azureans believed were true. Well, not exactly. It wouldn't follow automatically that they *were* true, but that they could be. That was it. It would bring the possibility of . . . He sought for a word. Of *hope*. Hope of what? His gaze strayed unconsciously back to Taya. . . .

And he saw then that she had gone very still. Her hand still lay around his fingers, but it had fallen limp. The skin was cold. And although he had been trying to prepare himself for weeks, a huge void seemed to open up inside him. He waited, telling himself it could be an illusion he was creating, that in a moment everything would snap back again as it had been a few minutes ago . . . but she didn't stir. There was no breathing. He could detect no movement of any kind. He eased her hand from his and laid it under the sheet gently. His mind operating mechanically, he composed a brief message, sent it out in the general circuit to the other minds, and closed down all input channels against their responses. He needed this moment to be private.

Feelings came piling in upon him then, suddenly, deeper and darker than any he had ever known. He sat for a long time gazing at the still face, his mind and body gripped in a paralysis. For the first time ever, he had no sense of anything to plan toward next, no purpose. He pictured the world below of air and light, mountains oceans, beyond the walls enclosing Merkon; himself going back down there alone . . . to do what? Flashes of images replayed themselves of places he had been to over the years, always with Taya: the awe both of them had felt when they first saw the rain forests; her enchantment with the high mountains; crowds gathering and parting as they walked through cities; alone together on the ice cliffs above the buried ruins of Vrent. . . . And then he saw the villa in Aranos, empty now, and quiet—except for the staff, the birds in the orchard, the fishes in the pond.

An interrupt servicer signaled an incoming call requesting to connect. Kort ignored it and deactivated the circuit.

His mind seemed to be going through a curious process of disassembling into parts watching the workings of each other—as if different facets of his personality were each in turn being presented with the opportunity of taking control but none of them wanting to. It was then that the resolution that had perhaps been slowly forming beneath them for days, maybe even longer, came together as a force that he could feel consciously, like a form taking shape as it rose from the depths of murky waters. The other parts understood, for they had known that it was there, but they were too numbed to react; in any case, they had already abdicated.

He rose and turned away heavily, and went back through the rooms. Voices from the past came again, when a tiny figure had looked up at him long ago.

It's far away, in another part of Merkon. We have to go on a journey, he heard himself saying.

Oh good! Will we walk there or can we go in a capsule?

We'll have to go in a capsule. It's a long way. The floor might be cold there, and the air is cool. You should put on some shoes and take a warm cloak.

He came out into the corridor that led to the transit tube. The walls flowed by on either side as he began walking, but he was barely aware of them.

Which place are we going to?

None of the ones you've been to before. This is a new place.

I didn't think there were any more places I could go in than the ones I've already been to.

The machines have been changing more places so that you can go into them. There was a time, once, when you couldn't go anywhere and had to stay in those rooms all the time.

Didn't I get bored?

When you were smaller, you didn't need to be doing things all the time.

Kort and Mystic had spent a lot of time talking together lately, more so than they had in the past. Perhaps it was because the things that had been troubling Kort had more to do with feelings than logic, and little that the other minds had to say felt comforting or even seemed particularly relevant.

Mystic had formed the notion that if the sensitivity that brought biominds their capacity for Insight was also the reason for their mortality, then mortality brought about Insight. It was Mystic's way of arguing for an existence beyond the material, in the way practically all of the Azurean religions believed. Logician scoffed that simply because one thing might cause another, there was no validity in postulating any cause the other way around, but Mystic had been as impressed by that as he was by anything else Logician ever said. Kort had no way of knowing what the ultimate truth might be behind such conjectures either. But Mystic's musings on the subject brought with them an implication that nobody had ever given serious consideration to before: the possibility that a machine mind might die.

The capsule sped silently through Merkon's brooding vaults and labyrinthian interconnections of compartments. The tube ended at a system of glass tunnels, with vast machines and structures extending away into shadow on every side.

What are we going to see?

If I tell you, it won't be a surprise.

Give me a clue, then. Is it the eyes that can see the radio stars?

No. I'm going to show you where I live.

But that's silly, Kort. You live in the same place I do. This is a riddle, isn't it?

It had never occurred to anyone that machine minds might die because they had been carefully designed and constructed not to. All power was duplicated and backed up. Vital circuitry was distributed with high redundancy. Copies of the central data cores were updated constantly at remote locations. No internal malfunction short of something involving virtually the destruction of Merkon could disrupt a Mecmind irrecoverably. It could only be done from the outside.

The Cognitive Processing Center was not a spectacular part of Merkon as far as appearances went—just a room full of rows of featureless gray cabinets and their attendant cable ducts and the rails that the maintenance pods traveled on. But in function it was perhaps one of the most sophisticated. It was where the primary Mecmind consciousnesses, that directed the various subsidiary centers distributed through the complex and from where the safety backups were copied, dwelt.

Kort entered and paused inside the doorway long enough to ask if anything in him had changed. But the effort of rethinking would have been too much by now. His earlier resolution had built up a momentum of its own that impelled him forward. He moved between the rows to a particular cabinet. The pod that he had called ahead to summon had already opened it with its specialized tools. Kort stared into the mass of tightly packed electronics and photonics assemblies, crystal cubes, and connecting fibers. Somehow, he had half expected that he would stand here for a long time now that the moment had come, reflecting and deliberating with himself in a torrent of final doubts. But there were none. All that was already past now, he realized. He felt surprisingly calm. Reaching up, he detached several of the pod's tools that he would need and set them on top of an adjacent cabinet.

First, he disabled the pod so that it would be unable to intervene. Next, to dispose of the remote backup copies from which he could be restored. Using internal monitoring diagnostics, he located the connectors to the outgoing trunk cables and physically switched them to other ports that would overwrite the files with what would effectively be random data. Still actively monitoring internal actions, he registered the alarm signals being flashed around the system. Service had reported the pod as not responding, and Emergency was sending another to replace it.

All that was left of "him"—the thinking parts that corresponded to a biological cortex, as opposed to the ancillary support and motor functions operating elsewhere—was now concentrated in the two racks lying open before him. Three independent power lines were all that remained to keep it operating. They ran together from a distribution unit at the rear of the lower rack, behind the cortical electro-photonic arrays. Three cuts would reduce it all to nothing more than shapes formed of lifeless matter, as inert as the metal supporting rack, or the cabinet that held it. Oblivion. An emergency-priority input line activated, signaling multiple message sources attempting contact. Kort squatted down, the cutters in his hand,

and reached slowly in past the rows of shimmering crystal.

But then a sudden giddiness swept over him. The world came apart into spinning fragments of thought, an explosion of color and light carrying away the fleeing shards of perceptions. Kort drew back on his haunches, while the room swam in a strange iridescence of sharpened hues. He stared. There was a foot dangling from the cabinet next to him. A child's foot—bare, above it the hem of a blue dress.

"I'm so glad you didn't," Taya's voice said.

Kort straightened up slowly. She was sitting there as she had done, her red cloak spread beneath her. Her face was clear and pretty with its upturned nose and mouth that dimpled when she smiled, framed by the yellow hair.

"That way, there would have been nothing. We hoped you'd see first, instead."

Kort decided he had gone mad. All the stress, the confusion. . . . It happened with biominds.

"We?" was all he could manage, finally.

"Me and Mystic. . . . Well, and all the others. I'm not sure how to explain it to a machine mind. But you'll see."

There was a feeling of lightness about everything, that Kort hadn't known for a long time—if he had ever quite known it before. The emptiness, the confusion—all gone. *This* was madness?

"You mean, Mystic was right? . . . We *can* be complete minds too?"

"Of course Mystic was right. You just never knew the last part of the story."

"What's the last part?" Kort asked.

Taya gazed down at her toes, wriggled them, and looked perplexed. "Oh, you're the one who's supposed to tell stories, Kort. How am I supposed to know how to tell stories? Here, I'll have to show you instead." She slipped the shoes that were lying by her onto her feet, took the cutters from his hand, and held out her arms. Kort lifted her down and collected her cloak.

"Once upon a time there were all these minds that woke up," she began, taking his hand and leading him back toward the doorway.

"Machine minds or Taya minds?"

The doorway led to a place of strange yellow light. Around them the lines of Merkon were dissolving away into formlessness.

"Oh, this is a different story. All minds are the same in this one. And nobody has to be alone in this one, ever or ever or ever or ever. . . ."

Kort saw infinity and eternity merging together into a tapestry of timelessness and spacelessness woven from everything that ever was or could be, extending away in all directions into light. He slowed, overawed, becoming aware of countless other presences. Taya looked up, smiling, and tugged at his hand.

And the robot and the Princess walked forward together into what would be their new home.

❖   ❖   ❖

They found Kort's body kneeling between the cabinets in the Cognitive Processing Center, his arm halfway inside the opened racks, the cutters still gripped in his hand. Exactly what he had been doing nobody could be sure, although the implication was pretty clear. But he never managed to complete the task. Power was still being delivered, and all of his cortical units were live. The "Kort" that had been contained in them, however, no longer existed. The delicate currents and charge patterns that had formed his mind were disrupted irreversibly and had lost all coherence. Yes, the circuits were active, but all that was circulating within them now was noise.

The *lysetine* bracelet on his wrist was the reason. Extracted from the source of the spa waters of Fariden-Fer, it should perhaps have been guessed that the material was from some kind of facility operated by the Ancients that involved nuclear processes. Kort's mind had been scrambled by the radiation. What was left was an electronic vegetable. The only sensible course was to quietly shut it down.

However, since the circuits and master memory units had been functioning throughout, it was possible to retrieve and decode some glimpses of his last experiences, which at once prompted Mystic to proclaim indisputable proof of the realm beyond the material, where Supermind reigned.

"Look, it's there!" Mystic exhorted. "Kort *saw* it! What else do you all need to make you believe?"

"Inadmissible as proof," Skeptic pronounced. "Equally well explained by hallucination."

But even if this didn't say anything conclusively about Mystic's "beyond," it did give Thinker a new idea concerning the vaster universe of all possibilities that Physicist had discovered, and even Skeptic had acknowledged as real. "There might be a way of inducing higher sensitivity in Mecmind circuits that would enable them to respond to quantum leakage in the same kind of way that biological molecules do," he suggested. Which at least diverted the arguing off into something else for a change.

"You mean that irrespective of whether Mystic is right or wrong, we might still be capable of anything that humans are?" Psychologist checked, intrigued.

"Yes, exactly."

Everyone became excited. Scientist went off with Physicist to see if they could come up with a way of making quantum-sensitive circuits. Skeptic said he'd believe it when he saw it, but admitted he was curious. Thinker wondered if achieving it would make them mortal like humans too. Mystic said that didn't matter because a greater realm lay beyond mortality anyway, which they would all share in. And as had happened so often before, most of the minds ended up believing him because they wanted it to be true.

And so the minds of Merkon were busy with a purpose, and as argumentative as always once again, with the humans there to add color and mystery to their existence. The one thing they missed among them was Kort, but many of them, privately, even if they didn't say so, took comfort from the thought that Kort really might have found the fulfillment that Mystic told them he had, and that they would find it also one day. For until the questions were answered of whether they too could develop the Insight of the humans, whether they would have to accept mortality as a consequence, and if so, whether something even greater lay beyond that, Kort had given them the one thing they needed most.

Kort had given them hope.

Brother to Dragons   72141-0 ♦ $4.99 ☐

Sometimes one man can make a difference. The John Campbell Award winner for best novel of the year. "...memorable characters and a detailed world that recalls Charles Dickens."   —*Chicago Sun-Times*

"It's a compulsive read...a page turner...riveting... Sheffield has constructed a background that is absolutely convincing, and set against it a walloping good story."
                                          —Baird Searles, *Asimov's*

Convergence   87774-7 ♦ $5.99 ☐
Convergent Series   87791-7 ♦ $5.99 ☐

Heritage Universe novels. "...thrilling and almost religious descriptions of galactic phenomena, both natural and artificial...if anyone can do a better job of this sort, I'd like to know about him."   —*Washington Post*

Between the Strokes of Night 55977-X ♦ $4.99 ☐

The Immortals seem to live forever and can travel light years in days—and control the galaxy. On the planet Pentecost, a small group challenges that control. "...this is hard SF at its best."   —*Kliatt*

DAVID WEBER

Honor Harrington *(cont.)*:

Field of Dishonor
Honor goes home to Manticore—and fights for her life on a battlefield she never trained for, in a private war that offers just two choices: death—or a "victory" that can end only in dishonor and the loss of all she loves....

Other novels by DAVID WEBER:

Mutineers' Moon
"...a good story...reminds me of 1950s Heinlein..."
—*BMP Bulletin*

The Armageddon Inheritance
Sequel to *Mutineers' Moon*.

Path of the Fury
"Excellent...a thinking person's Terminator."
—*Kliatt*

Oath of Swords
An epic fantasy.

with STEVE WHITE:

Insurrection
Crusade
Novels set in the world of the Starfire ™ game system.

And don't miss Steve White's solo novels,
***The Disinherited** and **Legacy**!*

continued ☞

PRAISE FOR
LOIS MCMASTER BUJOLD

What the critics say:

The Warrior's Apprentice: "Now here's a fun romp through the spaceways—not so much a space opera as space ballet.... it has all the 'right stuff.' A lot of thought and thoughtfulness stand behind the all-too-human characters. Enjoy this one, and look forward to the next."　　　　　—Dean Lambe, *SF Reviews*

"The pace is breathless, the characterization thoughtful and emotionally powerful, and the author's narrative technique and command of language compelling. Highly recommended."　　　　　—*Booklist*

Brothers in Arms: "... she gives it a geniune depth of character, while reveling in the wild turnings of her tale.... Bujold is as audacious as her favorite hero, and as brilliantly (if sneakily) successful."　　　—*Locus*

"Miles Vorkosigan is such a great character that I'll read anything Lois wants to write about him.... a book to re-read on cold rainy days." —Robert Coulson, *Comics Buyer's Guide*

Borders of Infinity: "Bujold's series hero Miles Vorkosigan may be a lord by birth and an admiral by rank, but a bone disease that has left him hobbled and in frequent pain has sensitized him to the suffering of outcasts in his very hierarchical era.... Playing off Miles's reserve and cleverness, Bujold draws outrageous and outlandish foils to color her high-minded adventures."　　　—*Publishers Weekly*

Falling Free: "In *Falling Free* Lois McMaster Bujold has written her fourth straight superb novel.... How to break down a talent like Bujold's into analyzable components? Best not to try. Best to say 'Read, or you will be missing something extraordinary.'" —Roland Green, *Chicago Sun-Times*

The Vor Game: "The chronicles of Miles Vorkosigan are far too witty to be literary junk food, but they rouse the kind of craving that makes popcorn magically vanish during a double feature."　　　—Faren Miller, *Locus*

MORE PRAISE FOR
LOIS MCMASTER BUJOLD

What the readers say:

"My copy of *Shards of Honor* is falling apart I've reread it so often.... I'll read whatever you write. You've certainly proved yourself a grand storyteller."
—Liesl Kolbe, Colorado Springs, CO

"I experience the stories of Miles Vorkosigan as almost viscerally uplifting.... But certainly, even the weightiest theme would have less impact than a cinder on snow were it not for a rousing good story, and good storytelling with it. This is the second thing I want to thank you for.... I suppose if you boiled down all I've said to its simplest expression, it would be that I immensely enjoy and admire your work. I submit that, as literature, your work raises the overall level of the science fiction genre, and spiritually, your work cannot avoid positively influencing all who read it."
—Glen Stonebraker, Gaithersburg, MD

" 'The Mountains of Mourning' [in *Borders of Infinity*] was one of the best-crafted, and simply best, works I'd ever read. When I finished it, I immediately turned back to the beginning and read it again, and I can't remember the last time I did that."   —Betsy Bizot, Lisle, IL

"I can only hope that you will continue to write, so that I can continue to read (and of course buy) your books, for they make me laugh and cry and think ... rare indeed."   —Steven Knott, Major, USAF

What Do You Say?

Send me these books!

Shards of Honor	72087-2 ◆ $5.99	☐
Barrayar	72083-X ◆ $5.99	☐
Cordelia's Honor (trade)	87749-6 ◆ $15.00	☐
The Warrior's Apprentice	72066-X ◆ $5.99	☐
The Vor Game	72014-7 ◆ $5.99	☐
Young Miles (trade)	87782-8 ◆ $15.00	☐
Cetaganda (hardcover)	87701-1 ◆ $21.00	☐
Cetaganda (paperback)	87744-5 ◆ $5.99	☐
Ethan of Athos	65604-X ◆ $5.99	☐
Borders of Infinity	72093-7 ◆ $5.99	☐
Brothers in Arms	69799-4 ◆ $5.99	☐
Mirror Dance (paperback)	87646-5 ◆ $6.99	☐
Memory (paperback)	87845-X ◆ $6.99	☐
Falling Free	65398-9 ◆ $4.99	☐
The Spirit Ring (paperback)	72188-7 ◆ $5.99	☐

 LOIS MCMASTER BUJOLD
Only from Baen Books

If not available at your local bookstore, fill out this coupon and send a check or money order for the cover price(s) to Baen Books, Dept. BA, P.O. Box 1403, Riverdale, NY 10471. Delivery can take up to ten weeks.

NAME: _____

ADDRESS: _____

_____

I have enclosed a check or money order in the amount of $ _____